"Isn't it warm in here?"

she said, and took off the jacket of her linen suit.

"It is getting warm," I admitted.

"Have another drink," she said.

Suddenly from the window behind her came the sound of a footstep on gravel.

"Did you hear that?"

I nodded. "Were you expecting anyone?"

She shook her head. "I heard that same sound last night. I'm frightened." She took a deep breath and stared at me candidly. "Would you stay here with me tonight?"

"For cash? As a bodyguard?"

She looked at me coolly. "Naturally, what else? There are twin beds. You can push one into the alcove."

I undressed in the darkness and groped my way to the bed. My hand felt the edge and worked toward the center and came in contact with something warmer, firmer and smoother than a blanket. "Wrong bed?" I asked politely.

There was a soft, muffled sigh. "You ask too many questions!" she said.

million dollar tramp

William Campbell Gault

Adams Media
New York London Toronto Sydney New Delhi

Adams Media
An Imprint of Simon & Schuster, Inc.
57 Littlefield Street
Avon, Massachusetts 02322

For information about special discounts for bulk purchases, please contact Simon & Schuster Special Sales at 1-866-506-1949 or business@simonandschuster.com.

Manufactured in the United States of America

ISBN 978-1-4405-5796-5
ISBN 978-1-4405-3917-6 (ebook)

This work has been previously published in print format by: Fawcett Publications. Inc., New York, NY.

Chapter One

The address he'd given me was in a run-down district on Figueroa Street. The stairs leading to his second floor office were served by a doorway that opened off the street between a pawn shop and a doubtful cigar store.

There was a worn wooden handrail, slick with new varnish, and ancient wooden paneling on the walls below the handrail level. Above it, the walls were plaster and could have used a coat of paint.

I went up the steps, through the odor of new varnish and old dust, and paused at the top to see which way the numbers ran. His number, 206, was only a few yards to the right of where I stood.

HEIRS, INCORPORATED read the lettering on his door. And below it, PLEASE ENTER.

Usually, in this neighborhood, that portion simply read WALK IN. Willis Morley was making an admirable attempt to rise above his environment.

The name and the district had led me to expect some dry and emaciated old fogey, bent over a ledger, or greedily counting his money. Willis Morley was nothing like that. As I came into the small waiting room, I could see through the open doorway that led to his office; Morley was sitting behind his desk in there.

His face was round and pink and his hair snow white. His tweed suit held many colors but the predominant color seemed to be orange. He would have made a perfect

5

Santa Claus for a Hollywood bookie's Christmas party.

He smiled at me through the open doorway, and his bright blue eyes twinkled. He asked, "Mr. Puma?"

"At your service," I answered. "Mr. Morley?"

"Correct. Come in, Mr. Puma, and be seated." He stood up and held out his hand. His body matched his face, round and plump.

I went over to shake his hand and then sat in the chair on the customer's side of his desk. The office was clean. It looked clean and would have smelled clean, I was sure, if the window hadn't been open.

"Another smoggy day," he said, sitting down.

"Is there another kind?" I asked.

He smiled. "Not in Los Angeles, not any more." He leaned back in his chair and studied me candidly. "You come well recommended, Mr. Puma."

"I'm pretty good," I admitted. "Who recommended me?"

He named an attorney I knew.

I asked, "Are you an attorney, Mr. Morley?"

For the first time, he frowned. "Not exactly. I've—had a rather extensive legal education but I never achieved a degree in law. Do you only work for attorneys, Mr. Puma?"

I shook my head. "I—uh—I mean, the nature of your business intrigued me. Do you look for missing heirs?"

He nodded. "At times. Though that kind of work would comprise less than a third of my total income. I'm a loan broker, Mr. Puma. I lend money to needy heirs against the time when they will no longer be needy."

"I get it," I said. "You keep 'em living until their benefactor dies, is that it?"

For the second time, he frowned. "That was rather crudely put, but more or less describes my major service." His smile was thin. "I didn't plan to have you investigate *me*, Mr. Puma." He looked past me. "A good number of the heirs aren't waiting for anyone to die, of course. They are legatees whose legacies are due at some previously determined time in the future. There is little risk involved in a loan to borrowers in this category, naturally. The others . . ." He sighed.

I smiled. "The others pay a much higher interest rate."

6

"Certainly." He looked at me blandly. "Nobody is *forced* to come to me for money, Mr. Puma."

"You've got a point," I admitted. "In this—less rewarding third of your business, this search for missing heirs, I suppose you hire one of the large detective agencies, one of the national agencies?"

He nodded and stared at me.

I stared back.

He stood up and went over to close the window. "Damned smog," he said, his back to me.

I said, "Don't get the wrong idea. I can always use a day's work. But it does seem strange that you didn't phone that agency first." I paused. "Or maybe you did —and they were too reputable to handle it?"

He sat down again and looked at me without emotion. "I was warned that you were insolent and arrogant. Are you trying to prepare me for an exorbitant fee?"

I shook my head.

He picked up a slide rule from his desk and considered it, while he said, "Mr. Puma, there are several national detective agencies and hundreds of small ones"—he paused—"like yours. A number of them seem to be prospering. They wouldn't be unless their many clients had a reason for not taking their business to the police departments in their home towns."

"True enough," I agreed.

He took a deep breath. "Your reputation is not exactly —impeccable."

"By my standards, it is," I said. "I guess my standards are as good as most."

"I'm sure they are. And I'm sure I've had less trouble with the police than you have, Mr. Puma. So mine must be at least equal to yours. Wouldn't you call that a fair judgment?"

I grinned at him. "I guess. What's the slide rule for?"

He smiled. "I use it for figuring percentages. Very handy gadget. Shall we get down to business, Mr. Puma?"

"I'm all ears," I told him.

A girl was missing, he told me, a twenty-eight-year-old girl who was into him for almost forty thousand dollars. In seventeen months she would be thirty and come into her inheritance.

7

"And you get your forty grand," I said.

He nodded.

"Plus interest," I said, "and maybe interest on the interest, to say nothing of your broker's commission. That could be quite a package. That might take one hell of an inheritance."

He looked at me coldly, his lips pursed primly. "Are you moralizing, Mr. Puma?"

I shook my head. "I'm trying to get the picture. If the debt is bigger than the inheritance, she'd have reason to be missing."

He smiled. "Hardly. The total inheritance will be in excess of three million dollars. The first installment, due on her thirtieth birthday, will be almost a million dollars."

I sat back and stared at him.

He continued to smile. The room was quiet.

Then I said, "Why here? Why you?"

"I'm not following you," he said quietly.

"A girl with that kind of money due," I explained, "could go to—well, to some lending institution that undoubtedly charges less than I'm sure you do. Don't get me wrong; I'm not saying you're a crook or anything like that. But you sure as hell aren't working on six per cent."

He nodded.

"Or even a clean twenty per cent, by the time you get through working that slide rule," I continued. "Mr. Morley, it just doesn't figure."

He took a deep breath. "You're a puzzle to me. I didn't phone you for an auditing; I phoned you as a prospective client. I'll say good-bye to you now, Mr. Puma. You obviously don't want my business."

I stared at him for a few seconds and then stood up. I said, "I need the business. I need it real bad this month. But I don't go into any job blind."

It was quiet again, except for the traffic noises from below. Finally, he said, "I'm asking you to find a girl. You're worried about how much interest she will pay. What business is that of yours?"

"None," I said. "I wasn't thinking of that. I was simply wondering *why* she came to you for money."

He took another breath. "Because she was fed up with all the red tape the banks go through in processing a loan.

8

And she was introduced to me through a mutual friend."

"Okay," I said. "Do you want to give me her name now?"

"Are you going to take the job?"

I nodded.

"Her name," he said, "is Fidelia Sherwood."

He had me staring again. It was a big family in this town, old and respected. Fidelia had been a blot on the family shield, married to a bogus count at nineteen, to a jazz pianist at twenty-four. She had divorced the pianist two years ago and had only recently been named as a correspondent in a rather messy Hollywood divorce action.

"Brother!" I said, finally.

Chubby little Willis Morley smiled smugly. He handed me a note-sized sheet of paper. "Here's a list of places she's been found before when she was—missing. It might be helpful."

I took the list and he added, "And here's a letter I want you to give her when you find her."

The letter was in a heavy, legal-sized envelope, sealed with red wax. He knew my rates and I knew as much as he wanted to tell me about his business. I took the letter and left.

The girl was probably not missing in the legal sense. She hadn't been in touch with him lately and was not available at home, and he was understandably worried. If she had owed me forty thousand, I'd have been worried, too.

I went down the steps through the odor of dust and varnish, thinking about Fidelia Sherwood, trying to remember all I had read about her in the newspapers. She had never lacked for publicity.

She was a willful girl, that much seemed certain, even discounting the exaggerations of newspaper feature stories. She was, or would be, an extremely wealthy girl; she was the only heir to the Sherwood money, so far as I had read. Her first husband, the fraudulent count, had graciously bowed out for a settlement reputed to be around a quarter of a million. Her second husband, a true American boy, had asked for no alimony.

It was now noon and I ate downtown. I came to the heart of this town so seldom I felt guilty about leaving

9

it without making some token purchase for the good of the Downtown Association.

I was glad I ate a full lunch. Because I had a very active afternoon, hitting all the spots Willis Morley had mentioned in his list. The area roughly called Los Angeles includes a lot of communities that aren't and some very remote neighborhoods that shouldn't be.

Nothing. Nobody had seen her and only one man seemed interested in my interest. He was a psychologist named Dr. Arnold Foy, who had a very swanky office on Wilshire. He was a *psychologist*, remember, not a *psychiatrist*, and I didn't know at the time how authentic that "Doctor" title was. In my town, anyone with two dollars and the first month's office rent can set himself up with a "Doctor of Psychology" sucker trap.

He was a tall man, thin and about thirty-five, soft-spoken and somehow superior, though perhaps he didn't mean to be. He was certainly a handsome bastard.

"Miss Sherwood missing again?" he said wearily. "Oh, God."

"You treated her, Doctor Foy?"

He dismissed the breach of etiquette with a smile. "How long has she been missing?"

"You tell me and I'll tell you," I said. "Did you treat her?"

"I'm a professional man," he said.

I shrugged. "So am I. You're not an MD, are you?"

His lean face stiffened. "It so happens I'm not." He studied me. "Are you implying that only MD's are permitted ethics?"

I smiled. "Not exactly. But I guess we both know how little it takes to hang up that 'psychologist' shingle. Maybe, between us, we have enough information to do Miss Sherwood some good. Let's not quibble."

He shook his head in dismissal. "I'm sorry, Mr. Puma, but I'm sure we have nothing further to discuss."

"We could talk about the Dodgers," I suggested.

He smiled his good-bye.

There was a possibility he was an honest man, but he left a bad taste in my mouth. It was five o'clock now, and the traffic on Wilshire was bumper to bumper and the air blue with smog. I walked to the nearest restaurant.

10

Two drinks and a slice of roast beef later, I drank my coffee and considered the last place on my list. It was a bar, way out near the beach, on the border between Santa Monica and Venice. I'd had a busy day through Los Angeles traffic and I was aching to get home, but my professional conscience drove me west, toward the ocean.

The name of the place was "Eddie's," a piano bar struggling for respectability in an area overrun with pansy beds. There were a couple of the lavender lads in a corner booth, giggling together, when I came in.

Behind the bar, the big man in the white jacket looked sour. He studied me doubtfully.

I shook my head. "I'm one of the virile ones. Are you the boss?"

He nodded. "I'm Eddie. Those guys in the corner bother you, I can bounce 'em. I'm looking for an excuse."

"They don't bother me," I said. "I'm looking for a woman named Fidelia Sherwood. Has she been in lately?"

"Last night," he answered. "She'll be in again, probably." He looked at the clock behind the bar. "In about twenty minutes, I'd guess, if you want to wait."

"I'll wait. I'll have a bourbon and water."

He set the drink on the bar and glanced annoyedly at the corner booth. "I try to keep 'em out. They keep all the good trade away." He sighed. "Every dime I own is tied up in this joint. I know now why I got it cheap."

I nodded sympathetically and glanced at the piano, a baby grand, on the stage set into the far curve of the bar.

The bartender must have misread my glance. Because he said, "Pete'll be in soon. Maybe they'll come together."

"Pete?" I asked blankly.

"Pete Richards," he explained. "Why do you think she hangs around here?"

Pete Richards . . . Ah, yes, the second husband, the pianist. "Oh," I said. "Oh, yes, of course."

"You looking for him, or her?" he asked me.

"Her," I answered, and showed him the wax-sealed envelope.

He frowned. "Summons?"

"No," I said, and then realized I couldn't be sure. "I doubt it," I corrected myself. "How long has Richards been working here?"

11

"Since he went on the booze, again. About a month. Nobody else will have him when he's on the booze."

"An alcoholic, eh?"

The big man shook his head. "I don't think so. Just one of them compulsive drinkers; he can always navigate. I'm not much for this progressive stuff, but his piano is okay with me."

"He's about like Shearing, maybe?" I asked.

"About," he said, and smiled cynically. "And cheaper. When he's on the booze, anyway."

"Does Miss Sherwood drink heavily?"

"Richards," he said. "Her name is Richards. Her divorce didn't change that."

"All right. Does Mrs. Richards drink heavily?"

He looked at the bar. "Maybe you'd better ask her that when she comes in. I don't yak about my customers."

His attitude had cooled in the last minute. I held his gaze and asked, "Did I say something wrong?"

"No." He took a deep breath. "You're a private eye, right? Your name Puma?"

I nodded. "And you don't like private investigators?"

He shrugged. "I don't like to yak about my customers with 'em."

I ordered another drink and said no more. A couple came in and took the booth next to the gigglers. One of the gigglers said, "Tourists," loud enough to be heard at the bar.

The bartender stared at them for seconds, and then went over to take the couple's order.

A girl came in, glanced quickly at the piano, and then came over to climb onto a stool in front of the bar. Her hair was between chestnut and auburn, her eyes a greenish-blue, her figure firm and slim and proud. She was wearing a light-green linen suit.

"Miss Fidelia Sherwood?" I asked.

"Fidelia Richards," she said, and looked at me without interest.

I slid the letter across the bar toward her. "From Willis Morley. He's worried about you."

From behind me, one of the weirdies in the corner called, "Fidelia, darling, come over and sit with us!"

She glanced their way, waved, and shook her head.

12

She looked back at me. "Do you work for little Willis?"

"Just for today. My day is done. Mr. Morley will want your new address. I think you'd better play along with him. You see, the law is on his side."

She picked up the envelope and tapped it on the bar. She smiled and said nothing. I sipped my second drink and lighted a cigarette.

The gay, gay, gay voice behind me called, "Come over here, Fidelia. We're certainly better company than *that!*"

The hair on my neck bristled, but I didn't turn around. They were sick, I told myself; they had their problems. But why did they have to be vocal?

Fidelia smiled sadly and then the big man came around behind the bar again and she ordered a Scotch on the rocks. "Pete's late," she added.

He turned to look at the clock, nodded, and fixed her drink. I sipped mine and stared at nothing.

The bartender told me, "No trouble, understand? I don't like 'em, but they're paying cash tonight."

I nodded.

Fidelia Sherwood Richards said, "You're Joseph Puma, aren't you? You're a friend of Mona Greene's."

"I was," I admitted. "Is she still in Italy?"

She nodded. "And happy. Married and happy. She's expecting a baby, and she's a little worried about that. She's thirty-nine, you know."

"I know. Mrs. Richards, you will get in touch with Willis Morley, won't you?"

She held up three fingers. "On my scout's honor. I don't know why he should be worried. When things pile up I always hide out for a while. This isn't the first time."

"Do you want to give me your present address," I asked, "to take back to him?"

"The Avalon Beach," she told me. "Do you know where that is?"

"I do. Will you be there long?"

"I'll be there tonight."

Again, the door opened. The man who came in was young-looking, but he was the kind who always would be. He had an attractively weak face and a crew cut and lustrous brown eyes, now bloodshot.

He stood next to Fidelia and they exchanged some

13

words too low for me to hear. Then he walked over to the piano.

I finished my drink and said to Fidelia, "Please get in touch with Mr. Morley, won't you?" I started to get off the stool.

"Wait," she said. "I want you to hear him."

I ordered another drink and settled back.

He was a little beyond me. Shearing's about my limit. The mild Shearing. This was more intricate, and occasionally, to my untrained ear, dissonant. Maybe it was meant to be.

Others drifted in, a few beatniks and some washed people and a few who looked like they were brothers of the duo in the corner booth. Another bartender had joined the boss and they kept busy.

I had no place to go but home, so I drank and listened. Maybe it was the alcohol. Or maybe it was the fact that Fidelia Sherwood Richards had moved over to take the stool next to mine and I could smell her expensive perfume.

At any rate, the piano of Pete Richards began to get through to me; I felt an empathy for Richards.

Next to me, Fidelia moved closer and asked, "Is he coming through?"

"Something is," I admitted, "though I'm musically illiterate."

"He's complicated," she said. "He's as complicated as Bach."

And then a big, white hand came from somewhere and rested on hers, and a petulant voice said, "Fidelia, I *insist* that you join us."

I turned to face the bigger of the two men who had been in the booth. He had looked big enough sitting down. Standing, I could see he was a giant.

He blotted out the rest of the room. He wore an Italian silk suit, black as sin, and a fawn-gray silk shirt and the insolent smile of the oversized noncomformist.

A tremor moved through me and I said, "Don't be pushy. Miss Sherwood is comfortable right where she is."

He moved in closer, crowding between us. The tremor in me was stronger now, and I tried to control it. I put a hand on his arm.

14

He turned to appraise me.

I said, "I promised the bartender I wouldn't start a fight. Don't make me break a promise."

He smiled. "Run along, process server; you've done your duty." He moved in toward the bar, and my stool began to teeter.

I put a forearm across his chest and shoved him back.

His big, white hand came swinging across the bar to slap my face, and I started to go over backward with the stool. I jumped in time, landing with my feet well spread as the stool clattered to the floor.

It wasn't a very bright thing to do, but I swung the right hand as soon as my feet were solid. It landed high on his cheek.

His head twisted and he stumbled into the bar. A woman screamed and somebody grabbed my arm and the big pansy swung from outer space.

I ducked, he missed, and I came forward to put the top of my head into his beefy face.

Now both bartenders were between us and a few of the customers had come over to help them. My tormentor and I stood a few feet apart, glaring at each other over the heads of the people between. Blood dribbled down from his nose and from a gashed lip, and his eyes were murderous.

The boss, Eddie, said, "You leave now, Puma. He'll leave in a couple of minutes. Unless you want me to call the law."

"I'm on the way," I said. "This is more his kind of place, anyway." I shrugged free of the men holding me and started for the door.

"Wait," Fidelia called, and I turned to see her worming through the crowd. "Wait for me."

I felt warm. It wasn't much of a conquest to have her leave the pansy for me, but it was encouraging to think she would leave the ex-husband she admired so much.

I waited at the door and we went out together. It was dark now, a clear, fairly warm night. She took a deep breath and stared up at me.

"You must have a car," I said. "It's impossible to live in this town without a car. Why do you need me?"

"I don't need you," she said. "I don't need anybody; it's one of my vices. And I have a car. But not here. I came in a cab."

"Now, why would you do that, Miss Sherwood, if you have a car?"

"Because I have another vice," she answered. "Alcohol. At times. And I don't like to drive when I'm drunk."

I stared at her and she stared at me and we thought our separate thoughts. I doubt if hers were as vulgar as mine. Finally she said, "Don't call me Miss Sherwood."

"Okay, Mrs. Richards."

"Call me Fidelia," she said. "Do you know what it means?"

"Hell, yes," I said. "Any Latin knows that. It means *faithful.*"

Chapter Two

I held the door open for her and she climbed into my weary Plymouth.

I started the engine and asked, "Where to?"

"We could go to the hotel and have a drink," she suggested.

That sounded innocent enough. I could put it on the expense account for Willis Morley; he would probably add fifty per cent and charge it to Fidelia.

At the next corner, I swung in a U-turn and headed back toward Santa Monica and the Avalon Beach. It was a fine hotel, with two excellent restaurants and a first-rate bar, and perhaps Fidelia and I could get to know each other.

If we got to be really intimate, perhaps I wouldn't even put the drinks on the expense account. I can be big, if the moment warrants it.

The U-turn had brought us back toward "Eddie's" again, and we were going by as Eddie escorted my recent opponent to the curb. The other bartender was along for protection.

"*Some* friends you have," I said, as we drove by.

16

She said nothing.

"A nice girl like you," I went on, "from a big family, hanging around that crummy bar with the lace underwear boys."

"They're all right," she said quietly. "They have their problems, even as you and I. Don't be obnoxiously virile, Joe Puma. I understand it's one of your major flaws."

"From Mona Greene, maybe? I did a lot for that girl. I straightened her out."

"Woman," Fidelia corrected me. "She's thirty-nine years old."

"She was only thirty-seven when I knew her," I said, "and she was extremely girlish."

Fidelia chuckled and asked, "Could I have a cigarette?"

I handed her my pack and some matches as we turned into Olympic. "Why would Mona Greene discuss me with you?" I asked. "I only really knew her for three days."

"They must have been very important days to her. She told me they changed the course of her life."

I said nothing. Mona had gone from me to Naples and there married that Neapolitan lover of hers. Mona Greene was one woman who had found me vulnerable.

I turned into Ocean Front, heading for the Avalon Beach. She said, "The driveway is about half a block from here. You'll see it soon."

"I know where the driveway is," I said. "It's at the next corner."

"For the hotel," she corrected me. "I have one of the cottages and that driveway is . . . right here."

I jammed the brakes and swung sharply to the right. When she had suggested a drink, innocent Joe Puma had assumed she meant at the bar. She had meant her cottage, a long, safe way from the registry desk of the main building. I felt a pressure mounting within me.

The juniper-edged driveway twisted and turned through the palm trees that shadowed the immense lawn. I said nothing. I was afraid my voice would be shaky.

She said softly, "Take the right turn at the next fork."

We went past a bungalow throwing a noisy party and past one where the lights were dim to one where the lights were out.

17

"Here," she said.

I pulled in next to a Corvette and turned off the engine. In the dim light of a distant yard lamp, she looked up and smiled.

I smiled. Neither of us said anything for a few seconds.

"Don't get any ideas," she said. "I only brought you here for a drink and some conversation."

"I'm not aggressive," I assured her. "Any ideas will have to be yours. I just hate to turn down free booze."

She continued to smile. "Of course," she said.

The cottage was low, board and batten, with a shake roof. Inside, it was paneled in mahogany, furnished in a pleasing shade of charcoal brown. There was a small sitting room off the bedroom alcove and a tiny but complete kitchenette.

She went into the kitchen to mix the drinks. I sat on a circular sofa near the television set. All the drapes were drawn; we were snug and alone.

A drink and some conversation. . . . Was that all she really wanted?

It seemed to be. She came back into the room to hand me my drink. She sat in a nearby chair and took a sip of hers. Then she said, "How did it happen that Willis Morley hired you?"

"I was recommended to him by an attorney we both know."

A silence, and I said, "How did it happen that you went to Willis Morley for money?"

"I saw his ad in the *Times*. It amused me. Don't you approve of Mr. Morley?"

I shrugged. "Even if I didn't, I wouldn't voice any disapproval. He was my client, today. He might be again." I took a drink and a deep breath. "However, this so-called Doctor Arnold Foy isn't my client and isn't likely to be. How did you ever get mixed up with *him?*"

She was rigid in her chair, staring at me. Her voice was tight. "What do you mean by the 'so-called' Doctor Arnold Foy?"

I said, "I'm always leary of people who use the title of 'Doctor' unless they've spent a lot of hard years earning it."

18

"Dr. Foy," she said evenly, "has been a godsend to me. Dr. Foy has kept me sane."

I smiled. "Okay. I apologize." I lifted my drink in salute.

"I'm sorry I suggested the drink," she said stiffly. "You're . . . impossible!"

"As soon as I finish it, I'll go," I said. "And I apologize for any implied criticism of Dr. Foy. We didn't hit it off in our little talk; I guess I'm too quick to resent an obvious superiority in another person."

She stared at her drink and at me. Finally, her chin lifted and she said, "And perhaps I'm too quick to defend him. Others have . . . talked against him, including all the physicians and psychiatrists I know."

"If he's done you some good," I said, "it doesn't matter much what others think. For you, then, he's automatically right."

She nodded and smiled sadly. "You don't have to go. Have another drink."

I took her glass with me and went out to the kitchen. I mixed a very pale pair of drinks and came back to hand her hers.

She looked at it and said, "You're being economical with my liquor, aren't you?"

"You drank quite a lot at Eddie's," I explained, "and so did I. You said you wanted to talk."

"I probably didn't," she said, "but it was the genteel thing to say."

Ouch! What did I do now, move in like some gauche Lothario? I laughed, and then said, "If Dr. Foy has spent all those fifty-minute hours making you genteel, he's wasted your money. Gentility is a monstrous middle-class goal."

She laughed, too. She lifted her drink and said, "Well spoken, professional peasant. Take this back and put some booze in it."

So, a start. But there were ethics involved now. I will not take advantage of a drunken woman. But her speech never slurred, nor did her mind slacken.

She told me about Dr. Foy. He had *released* her—that was the verb she used. It is used too much. She

19

meant he had released her from her inhibitions, but what he had probably done was release her from her conscience. Another word the quacks love is "free," but it doesn't describe the cost of their treatment.

She was free now; she was a free soul. Men love women who are free souls; so many of the quacks are men.

Some are half-men. I asked her, "Did you meet that big homo at Eddie's? Evidently, you knew him before tonight."

"I met him through Dr. Foy," she answered. "Brian is trying to overcome his . . . handicap."

"You met him through Dr. Foy? Is it just a coincidence that he hangs around the same bar you do?"

"You're being a detective," she accused me.

I shrugged.

She said, "Brian introduced me to Eddie's place. And I talked Eddie into hiring Pete until he comes out of this current siege."

I asked her quietly, "Do you still love him?"

"His piano," she said. "His talent, that's all." She stood up and took off the jacket of her linen suit. "Isn't it warm in here?"

Under the thin blouse, the firm lift of her breasts was sharply outlined. "It's getting warm," I admitted.

The pressure I had felt in the car was subsiding. She was flawed, she was vulnerable. It's no conquest when it's no contest.

"You're quiet," she said.

"I'm thinking of you, Fidelia Sherwood Richards. Rich and smart and pretty—what makes you so restless?"

"Dr. Foy says I'm seeking an impossible ideal. I suppose he means a man."

From the window behind her, there came the sound of a footstep on gravel, and she glanced quickly around, but the drape was drawn.

"Did you hear that?" she asked.

I nodded. I rose and went to the door. I turned on the outside light and looked around. Nobody was in sight.

I came back and asked, "Were you expecting anyone?"

She shook her head, staring at me. "I heard that same sound last night. I'm . . . frightened."

20

"It sounded like a footstep on gravel," I said.

She nodded. "And there's no gravel out there." She took a deep breath and stared at me candidly. "Would you stay here tonight?"

"For cash, I will——as a bodyguard."

Her face stiffened and she glared at me.

I said gently, "Don't you get the point? If you pay me money for staying here, there is no obligation on your part to pay me in any coin beyond money. You will be a free soul and any further payment you might contemplate will be purely of our own volition."

She continued to stare. Then she smiled, and then she laughed. And then asked, "How much?"

"One dollar," I said. And thought, *and other valuable considerations.*

It's a strange, damned thing. I come into contact with a lot of wealthy people because no other kind can afford my rates. And it's a strange damned thing how many of them are unhappy. Neurotic, obsessed, frustrated, restless, guilt-ridden.

What in hell does a man (or woman) need? Food, shelter, clothes, a few laughs and the proper enjoyment of the bed. What else is there? If you think there is anything else, you are overeducated or underage.

I said, "It's a strange damned thing."

"What is?" she asked.

"The number of wealthy people who are unhappy. It seems to be chronic among the rich."

"I'm not unhappy," she said, "not since I met Dr. Foy."

I thought, *if you think Foy's got it, wait until you really know Puma. You'll throw rocks at Foy.*

"What are you thinking?" she asked.

"The same as before——it's a strange damned thing."

"Have another drink," she said, "and don't worry about me."

It was acceptable advice. We drank. We didn't get drunk, but we got friendly. And when it was time to go to bed, we put one of the twin beds into the main room and left the other in the alcove.

She took a dollar from her purse and gave it to me and I put it into my wallet. She was a free soul now. And what was I? Underpaid.

21

She turned off the lights and went into the bathroom to undress.

I lay on my bed in the dark alcove, thinking back on the day, beginning with my visit to cherubic Willis Morley just before lunch. It had been a day full of incident, revealing a sketchy pattern of tangled lines. Foy to Brian (through Fidelia) to Eddie's (where Richards worked because of Brian to Eddie and Fidelia) to Richards.

There was a gap in it, somewhere. I listened to the sound of her shower and looked for the gap. It eluded me. Why did I have to play detective? My day was behind me; I had consummated the terms of my verbal contract with Willis Morley.

The sound of her shower continued and I thought of the dollar in my wallet and the footstep on the non-existent gravel and the fine line of her firm bosom.

The sound of her shower stopped and I thought I heard that footstep outside again. I didn't get up to investigate. My day was behind me, a night of semi-promise was ahead.

She turned off the light in the bathroom before coming out, so I got no glimpse of her. I heard her pad past and then the rustle of sheets on her bed.

I went to the bathroom consoling myself with the rationalization that I really needed a night of uninterrupted sleep. You can't win 'em all.

I came out twenty minutes later, and groped toward my bed. My hand felt the edge and worked toward the center and came into contact with something smoother, firmer and finer than a blanket. Her skin was smooth and warm; the delicate mist of her perfume bathed my nostrils.

"Wrong bed?" I asked politely.

"If that's a question, no," she answered. "If it's an accusation, I'll move."

It was a question, I told her, a meaningless question.

It was all tactile, the room completely without light. The tautness of her nipples, the flatness of her stomach, the action of her loins and the fullness of her buttocks— it was all tactile. Until the half-stifled cry of her climax and the satisfied sigh of fulfillment, it was tactile.

And then she said, "I'm too tired to move. You'll have to sleep in the other bed."

I groped my way to the other bed and crawled in.

I was stretching when she said softly, "Tell me about Mona Greene."

"There's nothing to tell," I answered. "I don't even remember her." I turned over. "Go to sleep, Fidelia."

"Beast!" she said, and laughed quietly. "Good night."

It was still dark when I wakened. Those were *some* drapes. It was nine o'clock in the morning and still dark.

And then the lamp next to Fidelia's bed went on and she rose, naked as ultimate truth.

I stared at her and she smiled back at me. "I'm never maidenly in the morning. Now, why is that?"

"You'd have to ask Dr. Foy," I said. "What time does the maid usually come in?"

"When I call for her. Will you go out and get the paper? I'll make some breakfast."

I slid into some pants and went to the front door. I opened it a crack first, to see if we had nosey neighbors, but we were well shielded by shrubbery from the next cottage.

There was no paper in sight and I opened the door wider to examine the yard. I saw it then, over near the street corner of the cottage.

As I started out, I heard that sound again, the footstep on gravel. I looked up and saw it was the dry frond of a palm tree scraping the rough eave edge of the shake roof.

I went past it to pick up the morning *Times*. And as I bent over, I saw the pair of feet. They were big feet. The body was obscured by the corner of the building.

I went around the corner and saw it was a big body too, the body of the man named Brian, my assailant of last night. There was no doubt that he was dead.

Chapter Three

In the cottage, Fidelia shuddered as I told her what I had found outside. She sat down on the divan, her legs wobbly, her hands trembling.

"It's no time to collapse," I warned her. "I'm going

23

to drive around the block, to warm up the engine on my car. While I'm gone, make one of those beds, but leave the other rumpled. Then I'll come back and phone the police."

She clasped her hands tightly in her lap and stared at the floor. She looked sick.

"Everything is the same as it happened," I explained carefully, "except that I wasn't here last night. I left after taking you home last night and came back this morning to check on whether you had phoned Willis Morley. That last is weak, but what else have we got? *Look at me, Fidelia!*"

She stared up at me blankly.

"That's our story," I said, "unless you want the papers to crucify us. Your reputation is at stake, and my neck."

"My reputation?" she said hoarsely. Her smile was ironic.

"Okay, then, think of my neck. Remember that I had a hassle with that man last night."

She inhaled deeply and stood up. "We'd better move that one bed back to where it was, or the maid will notice. I'll need help with that."

I helped her with the bed and then went out to my car. We were fairly well screened from the other cottages, but there was no way of being sure I couldn't be seen. If I simply started the engine and let it run for a while, it would be warm enough. But if I drove out and wasn't seen, and then drove back in, making enough noise, perhaps some gullible would confirm that I had arrived immediately before we phoned the police.

I wasn't acting like a solid citizen, but I had spent enough time in the L.A.P.D. to know what can happen occasionally to solid citizens. And this would be handled by the Santa Monica Police Department, where I had very few, if any, friends.

As far as I could tell, nobody saw me leave. This cottage was close to the lateral street and a service road led to it from our parking area.

I made a four-block swing, a total run of sixteen blocks, and had to wait for three lights. My temperature indicator showed a warm engine when I returned to the cottage.

There, as I drove past the cottage that had held the

24

noisy party last night, I killed the engine. I ground the starter and managed to tootle the horn before getting under way again. It had been necessary to over-choke the engine by pumping the accelerator to prevent its starting too soon, and a big cloud of unignited gasoline belched out as the engine finally roared into life.

From the noisy cottage, somebody yelled, "What the hell is going on out there?"

A man appeared in the doorway and glared over at me as I stepped from the Plymouth in front of Fidelia's cottage.

I made a one-act play out of ringing her door chime. Our neighbor was still glaring when Fidelia opened the door.

"It wasn't locked," she said nervously.

"I know," I said. "I'm working for an Academy Award." I went directly to the phone.

Sergeant Dan Loepke and Detective Mel Braun came over from Santa Monica Headquarters. Mel was a sort of half-friend of mine, but Sergeant Loepke and I were chilly acquaintances.

The Sergeant listened coolly and carefully to my story while Mel talked quietly with Fidelia out of earshot. I had a hunch they were going to check us against each other.

When I had finished, Loepke asked, "Know the man who was killed?"

I nodded. "I know his first name. It's Brian. I——had a little run-in with him last night."

His gray eyes showed interest. "Oh? Here?"

"No. At 'Eddie's'." I detailed it, favoring myself, natch.

"Hmmm," he said. "Stay here." He went over toward Detective Braun.

I watched him talk with Fidelia, and then looked through the window to see the boys carrying the body of Brian away. I was in the kitchen, getting a drink of water, when Loepke rejoined me.

"This Brian Delsy," he asked, "when did you *first* meet him?"

"Last night, Sergeant."

He stood there and stared at me, a fairly short, heavy,

solid hunk of mean cop, an old pro, cynical and efficient.

I returned his gaze.

He expelled his breath and came over to get a glass of water. His back was to me when he said, "You'll come along with us. Maybe, down at the station, you'll think of something you haven't told me."

I said nothing.

He drank and turned around. "That Delsy was *shot*, Puma, shot with a .38."

"So?"

"So nobody heard a shot around here, according to the officer who just checked the neighbors. A .38 makes a pretty fair noise, wouldn't you say?"

"Right. So?"

"So dumping that body here looks like the cheap kind of trick a private eye might pull to put the screws to somebody as rich as Fidelia Sherwood."

I stared at him. Anger stirred in me, but I fought it. I said, "I'll phone my attorney from here, if you don't mind."

"I mind," he said. "Come on along."

I followed him from the kitchen. In the living room, I stopped to tell Fidelia, "Call my attorney, Joseph Devlin in Beverly Hills, and tell him to send somebody down to the Santa Monica Headquarters with bail or a writ or whatever he might need."

The Sergeant stopped short of the door and turned slowly. He said quietly, "You don't want any trouble, Miss Sherwood. Forget this peeper opened his mouth."

"My name is Richards," she said, *"Mrs.* Richards."

"Is it, now?" he said. "At the desk, they told one of my men you were registered as Miss Fidelia Sherwood."

"I've always used that name here," she said. "Ever since I *was* Fidelia Sherwood." She looked at me. "Perhaps I'd better send my attorney, Mr. Puma. He's very well known in this town. He's a brother of the Mayor."

The Mayor had only one brother, a former governor of the state. I smiled and said, "I've heard that Fidelia means faithful."

She smiled back. "I'm in your corner, Mr. Puma."

I could almost see the smoke as Sergeant Loepke stood near the doorway and smouldered. His voice was hoarse

26

and ugly. "I think you both had better come to Head-quarters."

Mel Braun said hesitantly, "Sergeant, Joe—I mean Mr. Puma—has a reputation for insolence but also one for exceptional honesty as regards—"

"I didn't ask for any character references, Officer. Let's go—both of you."

"As soon as I phone," Fidelia said. She walked over and picked up the receiver.

Loepke muttered something and moved swiftly across the carpeting to fasten a fat hand on her wrist.

Nobody moved. Braun started to speak, and stopped. Fidelia stared at the hand on her wrist and the blue-green eyes were cold and withdrawn.

Braun said, "Easy does it, Sergeant."

Fidelia's voice was tight, almost shrill. "Take your hand away, Sergeant, or I'll scratch your eyes out."

"Are you coming along?" he asked. "Are you coming quietly?"

"It's not the right time to make an issue of it, Mrs. Richards," I said. "Let's go quietly."

She looked at me as Loepke took his hand off her wrist. She didn't move.

"We have to learn to adjust to the unreasonable. It's an unreasonable world," I said soothingly.

Loepke looked at me. "Is that a crack?"

I shook my head and met his gaze. "No, Sergeant." I took a deep breath. "Don't crowd your luck, Sergeant."

There was a static moment, and then Mel Braun said easily, "Shall I run them down, Sergeant, or do you want me to stay here?"

Loepke didn't look at him. "You stay here."

Loepke drove us down in the Department car. Nobody said a word. Fidelia stared out the window. I stared at the back of Loepke's neck and he kept his eyes on the traffic.

In the big building that overlooks the Bay, he took us to the office of Captain Aaron Amos. The Captain was a reasonable man; almost a friend of mine.

Loepke briefed him, and then added, "Mrs. Richards tried to intimidate me, sir. She dropped some names."

The alert face of Captain Amos tightened.

27

I said, "That's not true. The Sergeant tried to manhandle Mrs. Richards. And he accused me of killing Brian Delsy and then dumping his body near Mrs. Richards' cottage."

There was a big, fat silence—and then Fidelia chuckled.

The three of us looked at her. She smiled at Captain Amos and said, "The Sergeant didn't hurt me. It was a rather absurd situation all around, and better forgotten. What did you want from us, Captain?"

Amos studied her for a moment and then looked at Loepke.

Loepke said, "All I want is some truth, *polite* truth."

Captain Amos said, "Get officer Barker for dictation, Sergeant."

Loepke left and Amos looked sadly at me. "I suppose your big, loud mouth was working overtime, as usual?"

"No, sir. I was real cooperative."

"I'll bet." He looked at the closed door and back at me. "The Sergeant has been overlooked on two recent promotions. He's a good officer, Joe. Bitter, but first-rate."

"So, okay. I swear to you I didn't give him cause for his hysteria. I told him my story and he came up with this dumping-the-body bit. He must watch old movies on TV."

The Captain's eyebrows lifted. "*Somebody* dumped the body. Delsy wasn't shot where he was found."

"If the shot wasn't immediately fatal, he could have made his own way to the cottage, couldn't he? Or he could have been shot with a silencer. There wasn't the slightest damned reason in the world for Sergeant Loepke to dream up his idiotic fantasy."

"The shot was immediately fatal," Captain Aaron Amos said.

And then a uniformed officer came in to take our statements and Amos left the room. He wasn't back by the time we had finished and signed our statements.

Loepke came in to tell us we could go. And he hadn't quite cooled off. He told me, "One of these days, you'll slip. When you do, I hope it's here, in *my* town."

I said nothing.

28

Fidelia said quietly, "You need help, Sergeant. There are clinics where it's not expensive."

He began to smoulder again, glaring and rigid. I said, "That wasn't a crack. Mrs. Richards is serious. All of us need help one way or another, Sergeant."

"Get out of here," he said. "Both of you. Beat it."

Fidelia started to say more, but I had her arm and I pulled her quickly away from there. Outside, I told her, "We got off very easily. We're still not clear. We don't need any more enemies than we have."

"Poof!" she said. "Policemen. Poof!"

A traffic officer drove us back to the Avalon Beach. There, Fidelia said, "You might as well stay for a late breakfast. I may decide to hire you."

"Hire me? For what?"

"Not what you're hoping. As an investigator. That is *one* of your services, isn't it?"

"Oh, boy!" I said. "We're adjusted now. You're back to dominance, aren't you?"

She kissed my cheek. "No. I'm going to serve you breakfast, aren't I? Joe, I have a rock in Dr. Foy. But I need a shield."

My lover's mind wanted to accept her explanation, but my working mind balked. She needed a shield? I had seen her under stress. I had seen her calmness in front of the police and after a man had been found dead not fifty feet from where we had slept.

"Don't look so cynical," she said. "Did the mention of Dr. Foy cause that look?"

"Maybe," I lied. "Maybe, unconsciously. It's almost noon; let's get going on that breakfast."

Her smile was wry. "Yes, master."

She fried me four eggs, sunny-side up, and toasted half a loaf of bread and broiled some ham a special way and served it with a barbecue sauce. And while we ate, we talked.

Had dad had died three years ago. Her mother had died just a week before Fidelia had sought the solicitude of Dr. Foy. Her mother's death, it seemed likely, had been the blow that had made Foy necessary.

"And now he's your rock," I said. "That's dangerous,

29

Fidelia. He can become so important to you you'll *never* be able to leave him."

"That's a danger," she admitted. "But I'm not ready to face it, yet."

I shook my head wearily. She looked sadly at the table.

I asked, "Is it trouble that makes people rich, or wealth that makes people troubled?"

She sipped her coffee and said nothing.

I thought of last night and remembered how soundly I had slept, right through, without rememberable dreams. She could have left the cottage while I was asleep, left the cottage and killed Brian Delsy.

"What are you thinking about?" she asked me.

"Nothing," I said.

"I was thinking," she said evenly, "that you could have left the cottage while I was asleep last night."

I stared at her.

"And you could have been thinking that about me," she said. "Were you, Joe?"

I lied with a shake of the head. "I was wondering why the administrator of your estate didn't warn you against Willis Morley."

"I didn't consult him. I have an allowance, you know —five hundred dollars a week. I'm supposed to live on that until my thirtieth birthday. That's seventeen months from now. I can't make it, not on five hundred a week."

"You can't afford me on five hundred dollars a week, either," I told her. "I get a hundred a day and expenses."

"I'll bet you didn't charge Mona Greene that."

"I charged her that and she paid me five times that," I answered. "In *money,* in case you're wondering."

"Don't be vulgar," she said. She sighed. "Couldn't you let me owe you? Or couldn't you explain to the attorney in charge of the estate that finding the murderer of Brian Delsy is important to my safety?"

"You could owe me," I agreed. "Trying to explain to a lawyer why the normal processes of law aren't adequate would take more persuasion than I possess."

"You could do it," she urged. "You're very persuasive."

"Not around lawyers. Tell me, how well did you know Brian Delsy?"

30

She frowned. "As a casual friend. Why?"

"He died fifty feet from you," I said. "You don't think that was just a coincidence, do you?"

"We don't know where he actually died," she said. "The police said the body had been moved."

"All right, then," I said impatiently, "he was *found dead* fifty feet from here. Is *that* a coincidence?"

"I suppose not," she said. "Why are you so cross?"

"I'm nervous. You're not, and you're supposed to be. You're the girl who can't face reality and I'm the tough and cynical private eye and I'm breaking up while you sit there like a—"

"A rock?" she asked.

"Like a really adjusted citizen," I corrected her. "I think you need Dr. Foy about as much as I need a girdle."

She sipped her coffee.

I finished the toast and poured myself some coffee.

"I suppose," she said softly, "last night to you was just another—episode."

"The death of Brian Delsy, do you mean?" I asked.

Her chin lifted. "No, I don't mean the death of Brian."

I took a breath and looked at her. "Was it just an episode to you, Mrs. Richards? Aren't you going a little maidenly on me?"

She began to color, a flush coming up into her cheeks from her throat.

I studied her. "Was I vulgar again?"

She nodded.

"I cherish last night," I said. "But this is the morning, Fidelia, and a man is dead. Even if we aren't involved technically, we're involved as humans."

She began to cry quietly.

"Fifty dollars a day," I said, "and you can owe me. Special rates for special people. Where does your ex-husband live?"

"You monster!" she said chokingly.

I shook my head. "I'm your shield, remember? Does he live in Santa Monica?"

She rose quickly and left the table. I lighted a cigarette to go with the coffee and listened to the sound of water running in the bathroom. She was a strange one, but how

31

many women aren't? They don't live in a man's world.

When she came out again, her face had been washed and her eyes were clear. She looked at me gravely and I smiled at her.

"I don't know where he lives," she said, "but you won't need to look for him. He's the most . . . non-violent man I ever knew."

"I wasn't thinking of him as the killer," I explained. "But he must have been at Eddie's last night when Delsy left. Or he might have overheard something. Delsy wasn't alone when we left him, remember."

"No," she said. "Eddie was standing with him at the curb. But Bob wasn't around."

"Bob?" I asked. "Is he the other fellow who was in the booth?"

She nodded. "Bob Tampett." She spelled the last name for me. "Bob might know something." She gulped. "You're going to work on this—for me?"

I nodded. "At my special rate. But you're going to have to be honest with me, Fidelia, as honest as you are with Dr. Foy."

She licked her lips. "I will be. I need you, Joe."

Chapter Four

Oh, hell, yes. When there's dirty linen to be washed or rocks to be looked under, they always need me. But why didn't they need me when the sun was bright and the outlook fair?

I kissed her gently on the forehead and told her to be careful and went out to my wheezy steed. I had suggested that she find another motel or apartment, but she liked it here. It was familiar and she needed that much of a base at the moment.

So I promised her I'd report back before the sun went down and I went out and drove over to Venice, right across the border from Santa Monica. Venice is a part of Los Angeles; Santa Monica isn't. The police in Venice trusted me and they had reason to. I had helped them

32

in a messy case less than six months ago.

Eddie wasn't behind the bar. It was now one-thirty and he wasn't due until four. The bartender wasn't the same one who had worked with Eddie last night, so he knew nothing about the donnybrook. But he did have Pete Richards' address, and he gave it to me.

It was an apartment on lower Ashland Avenue. Richards wasn't home. And where did I go now?

From a drugstore, I phoned Willis Morley and told him I had delivered the letter. He told me Fidelia had phoned him and my check was already in the mail.

And then I thought of Robert Tampett and looked him up in the book. There was a possibility he wasn't a working man and would be home. I could have phoned, but I like to watch people's faces when I talk with them.

He was in the book. It was a Santa Monica address.

It was a two-story, twelve-unit apartment building of gray stucco and redwood, built around a pool, on Montana Avenue.

I went up the outside steps to the wrought-iron-guarded runway and down that to apartment eight. The door chimes played "taps." Tricky.

The piece wasn't finished when the door opened and a thin, hard-faced man of medium height and slender build stood there. His hair was cut short—wiry, thick hair. He looked rugged and not at all as I had expected, though I remembered him dimly from last night.

"Well?" he said.

"Robert Tampett?"

He nodded.

"Remember me?"

He nodded.

"I came to talk with you about Brian Delsy," I explained.

His face was bland, his gaze candid. "He's dead."

"I know. That's why I'm here. Do I come in or do we talk for the neighbors?"

He yawned. "Talk? About what?"

"About the death of your friend."

He looked at me contemptuously. "Beat it, muscles!"

I looked at him tolerantly. "I'll bet you're one of those little guys who studied judo, huh? I'll bet you watch TV

33

and see how the skinny, smooth heroes handle the beefy boys. I'll bet you don't even realize I could throw you from here to the pool with either hand."

He started to close the door.

I put a foot in the way of the door.

He looked at my foot, then at my face. His voice didn't sound frightened. "I'm not one of 'those little guys.' I'm not an outsized freak like you, but I'm not little. I've already talked with the police and you haven't any authority. If you want to wait here until I phone them, okay."

"I thought Mrs. Richards was a friend of yours," I said.

More interest in his eyes, but not his voice. "I know her."

"I'm working for her."

He studied me, chewing at one corner of his mouth. Then, "Okay if I phone her to check that?"

"Of course."

"What's her number?"

I told him it was the Avalon Beach and he closed the door and locked it before phoning. In a few minutes he came back to open the door again. He said, "Come in."

The furniture was new and modern, mostly upholstered in a buff Naugahyde. The prints on the walls were fair reproductions and an expensive-looking portable bar stood against the dining room wall.

"Do you work nights?" I asked him.

"Night and day," he answered. "Are we going to talk about me or about Brian?"

"Both, if you don't mind," I said. "Do you have a problem, too, Mr. Tampett?"

He stared at me coldly. "Talk English."

"Brian had a problem," I explained, "that Dr. Foy was trying to correct. I thought that might be where you met."

"It doesn't matter where we met," he said. "Last night is all you're interested in, isn't it?"

I sat in one of the Naugahyde pull-up chairs. "Not necessarily. Murder has to have some background. It requires motivation, or else it's manslaughter. This didn't look like manslaughter."

He opened a can of beer, but didn't offer me any. He took a deep swallow and said, "I knew Brian from

34

Eddie's. Last night, after Eddie bounced him, I hung around for a while and then came home. That's what I told the police. Why Fidelia should hire you to ask the same stupid questions is beyond me."

"Where did you meet her?"

"At Eddie's."

"What were you giggling about last night?"

His face hardened. "I wasn't giggling. I was talking to Brian. Maybe he was giggling, but I wasn't. When something strikes me funny, I *laugh*."

"That's the manly thing to do," I assured him. "How much money have you borrowed from Mrs. Richards?"

He glared and said hoarsely, "Not a goddamned dime! And she never told you I did."

"True enough," I admitted. "But you look like a hustler to me and I can't see you overlooking such a soft touch."

"Listen, peeper," he said grimly, "I didn't invite you in here to be insulted. And I don't have to hustle broads. I can always turn a buck, a damned sight better than you can."

"That's what I meant. You're a hustler. Admit it, Tampett. If not women, swishes. Right?"

He looked at the can of beer, as though intending to throw it at me.

"I'll take it back," I said, "if you want to tell me what you do for a living." I indicated the apartment around me. "It's a sure thing you don't work the night shift at Douglas."

"Beat it," he said. "Get out before I call the law."

"Calm down," I said soothingly. "I was just trying to annoy some truth out of you."

He walked over to the phone and lifted it. He said quietly, "You've got ten seconds."

"Call 'em," I said. "I'll tell them that you approached me on the street and invited me up here. That should get you ninety days, if you've got a record."

"One," he counted. "Two, three, four——"

I thought of Sergeant Loepke, of trying to explain my position to *him*. I thought of his threat. I rose and said, "Stop counting. I'm on the way." At the doorway, I turned. "But I'll be back, little man."

35

"I'm not little," he said hoarsely. "I'm not a freak, like you, but I'm not little. I'm almost five-ten, see, and you don't scare me a damned bit!"

"Don't get hysterical," I told him tolerantly. "I'm going." I closed the door quietly.

The latch had scarcely clicked before the beer can clattered against the other side of the door.

Robert Tampett had his problems, too. And one of them was that he was *almost* five-ten. I went down the steps conscious of my impressive size.

I drove over to Santa Monica Headquarters hoping that Mel Braun would be there. He wasn't, but another detective who liked me better than Loepke did was in, and cooperative.

They had no record on Robert Tampett.

"If he's a swish," my friend said, "and lived here long enough, we'd have something." He shook his head. "With that beach and canyon gang, they're a major problem here, let me tell you."

"I've a hunch," I said, "he's as normal as we are, but hangs around with the lavender lads. And that's worse, don't you think?"

He nodded, his eyes bleak.

I asked, "Anything new on Delsy's death?"

He shook his head. "I hear Loepke gave you a bad time."

I shrugged.

"A bitter man," he said. "A good officer but a hell of a sour man. Well, Joe, you get something, I can use it. This is a two-way street, you know. I can use help, too."

I promised to keep him in mind and went out. Again, I drove over to Ashland Avenue. This time, Pete Richards was home.

He was in the courtyard of the apartment building, in shorts and sneakers, soaking up the sun. And sweating out the booze, he told me. He'd been home when I had rung his bell before, but hadn't answered.

He offered me a glass of water from the pitcher of ice water on the grass next to him. As I drank, he said, "Back on the wagon, again. Man, that was some session I just went through."

36

"How long?" I asked.

"Six weeks," he answered.

"You worked all through it?"

He nodded. "At Eddie's. So I guess I wouldn't be a genuine alcoholic." He stretched, arching his neck. "I guess the law was here this morning and figured like you that I wasn't home. I saw an early afternoon paper." He made a face.

"I've just been over to see a man named Robert Tampett," I said. "Know him?"

He nodded. "Friend of that big queer—the one that got killed. I don't think Tampett's one, though."

"Neither do I," I agreed. "Did Tampett leave with Delsy last night?"

Richards looked thoughtful. "I—don't think so. . . . Wait." He screwed up his forehead. "There was somebody sitting in that booth with Tampett after Delsy was bounced. Tampett stayed for a while." He sighed. "I don't know how long, though."

"Was it a man or a woman who sat with Tampett?"

"A man," he said. "Tall, thin. Kind of an elegant gent."

"Do you know Dr. Foy?" I asked.

He shook his head. "I never met him. I heard enough about him through Fidelia."

A silence, and I asked, "Do you still love her?"

"I always will," he said simply. "I couldn't live with her; nobody can. But you *have* to love Fidelia if you're at all human." He smiled at me. "Don't you love her?"

I agreed I did. But added, "It doesn't mean much. I'm not discriminating. I love all females from eight to eighty."

His eyes were reminiscent. "She's never malicious. She's never petty or pretentious. In those ways, she's not anything like a woman."

If she's not a woman, I thought, *nobody ever was.*

I drank another glass of water and asked, "Who would want to frighten her or frame her? Who would have dumped the body of Brian Delsy so close to her cottage door?"

He closed his eyes and slowly shook his head. "I can't think of anybody. It had to be a coincidence. Unless . . .

37

do you think there's a possibility Brian was going over to see her, was shot on the way, and still tried to reach her?"

"No," I said. "Think! Certainly, she must have had *some* enemies."

"I'm trying to think," he said quietly. "I'm trying so hard it aches." He shook his head. "Nothing, nothing, nothing—"

"All right, then," I said, "who gains if she's discredited?"

"Nobody I know of," he said.

I stood up and thanked him. I started to leave, when he said, "Wait." He rubbed his forehead nervously. "That man who sat in the booth with Tampett after Brian left —I remember Fidelia mentioned his name to me once." He made a fist and hammered his forehead with a knuckle. "His first name is—Louis. That's it, Lou Serano."

Serano, Serano, Serano. The name went around in the card file in my brain and came up with something. I said, "There was a pusher named Serano, convicted of a narcotics violation. Could that be the man?"

Richards looked at me anxiously. "I've no idea. God!"

"Was Fidelia ever on the needle?"

He shook his head. "Not that I know of. I'm sure I'd know."

"Were you?" I asked.

He shook his head again. "Reefers, a couple of times, but never the needle. Booze is my problem." He belched and looked sickly at the grass. "Fidelia—she's a damned target! The publicity she's had and the people she hangs around with—it's criminal. They want to get into her and into her money."

He was so right. All towns are filled with predatory males, but this area attracted the real scum, the rootless, aggressive, immoral, crafty tigers who would never punch a time clock.

I went back to the Avalon Beach to check in with my lamb.

"What have you learned?" she asked.

"Nothing I didn't know," I answered. "Fidelia, what's their lure?"

"Whose lure?"

"The trash you associate with. They're out to cut you

38

up like a pie and divide you among them. What's wrong with your real friends?"

"They're dull," she said. "They stifle me."

"They can't all be dull," I argued. "At *every* social level, some people are dull and some aren't. Look for the ones who aren't."

She shook her head. "At the Sherwood level, they're *all* dull."

I sat on the bed and stared at her.

She said, "Bob Tampett called me to check on you. How did you two get along?"

"Badly. Why?"

"You're both so self-consciously aggressive," she said. "I thought there'd be sparks."

"He's a hoodlum," I said. "He hasn't any record I've been able to uncover, but I can smell a hoodlum and he has the odor."

"If he hasn't any record," she pointed out coolly, "you're judging him emotionally. Is that efficient police procedure?"

"I'm not a policeman," I explained slowly. "I'm a private investigator and I work by hunch. I work by hit and miss and trickery and throw my weight around. If you'd wanted a policeman, you wouldn't have hired me."

"All right," she said. "All right. Relax."

"Louis Serano," I asked. "Know him?"

She nodded.

"Is he the Serano with the Las Vegas tie-ups, the pusher?"

"I have no idea. He spends a lot of time in Las Vegas, I know."

"Do you, too?"

"When I was going through my gambling period. Dr. Foy cured me of that."

Natch. I thought. *He can use the money, himself.* I said nothing.

"You're dispirited," she said. "Why, Joe?"

"Because it's tough to help people who won't help themselves. It's—frustrating."

Her chin lifted. "That's not fair. Since I started going to Dr. Foy, I've seen less and less of those kind of people."

"You were involved in a divorce case just last month. You were named as correspondent, if I remember."

The flush in her cheeks again and the moisture in her eyes. "I thought I was in love. Can't you understand that? Damn you, hasn't it ever happened to you?"

"Yes," I said. "I'm sorry. Fidelia, don't cry. I'm sorry."

She sniffed. "I don't know Louis Serano well. Nor Bob Tampett either. I kept going to Eddie's place because Pete was playing there. Dr. Foy has slowly been weaning me away from those kind of people. I've got all of Pete's records, but the records aren't one-tenth as exciting as listening to him in person."

"Okay," I said soothingly. "I'm on your side, Fidelia."

"For fifty dollars a day you're on my side," she said.

I stared at her for seconds and she stared back.

"I'm a poor man," I finally said, "and I can't work for nothing. All right, you don't owe me a dime, and I'll say good-bye to you now."

Her smile was sad. "Even if I apologize?"

"Even if you apologize. In my business, I'm forced to walk a narrow, tricky road. And unless my client has complete faith and complete loyalty, I'm finished."

"I believe in you," she said.

"And complete honesty," I added. "That's more important than the rest."

"I'll be honest," she said. "But you must *believe* in me, too, Joe."

Her door chime sounded and she rose and went to the door. I heard the man say, "You and Puma will have to come down to the station, Mrs. Richards."

She opened the door wider and I saw it was Mel Braun.

"Now what, Mel?" I asked him.

He looked sheepish. "The Sergeant's been checking on last night." Mel looked at the floor. "You lied to him, Joe. You stayed here last night."

Chapter Five

Brother! I could see the headline. After my lecture about her disreputable playmates, the lecturer was going to be responsible for another Fidelia Sherwood headline.

40

I said to Mel, "The man's insane. What in hell is his beef with me? Why this persecution?"

"Let's go, Joe," he said quietly.

"I'll go," I said to Fidelia. "You stay here."

Mel shook his head. "Both of you. That's the order."

Fidelia said, "I'll change my shoes and be right with you. Please wait outside."

Mel flushed. I said quickly, "I'll wait with you, Mel. The lady has a right to some privacy, hasn't she?" I went out and closed the door behind me.

We stod there, saying nothing while we waited. Mel seemed embarrassed and I had a hunch he realized Sergeant Loepke was acting out of some personal animosity.

When Fidelia came out, Mel looked at her shoes and up at her. "I thought you were going to change them?"

"I decided to use the time to phone my attorney," she said. "Where's your car?"

It was now three-thirty. The sun was bright as we drove along Ocean Front and the Pacific was placid and a deep, rich blue today. Fidelia smoked and stared out the window; I planned words for Sergeant Loepke, placating words that would not be servile.

We waited for ten minutes in a small corridor at the rear of Headquarters until the great Loepke was ready to see us. Then we went into a room furnished with about a dozen folding chairs, a desk and three or four captain's chairs. Sergeant Daniel Loepke sat behind the desk, looking efficient and smug and mean.

"Well," he said, "I've got your *sworn* statements around here somewhere." He began to leaf through papers on his desk.

"Right on top there, Sergeant," I told him. "Try not to ham it up too much."

His eyes locked with mine and we glared at each other like adolescents. Then his gaze shifted to Fidelia. "Are you ready to admit you lied, Mrs. Richards?"

She yawned, and shook her head. She went over to one of the captain's chairs and sat down.

Loepke said, "There are some reporters waiting for another Fidelia Sherwood story. I don't know who alerted them."

"I can guess," I said. "And when Mrs. Richards sues,

41

her attorneys will undoubtedly sue you, personally, not the city. Because this persecution is personal, isn't it?"

"You watch your tongue, Puma," he said.

"I am. I'm not making any idle threats. The badge doesn't make you any kind of a *god*, Sergeant. You're just a public servant, like all the rest. And I'm a citizen."

"Not of this town, you're not. Now either shut your big mouth or I'll have you locked up until you learn some manners."

I stared at him; he glared at me. I could have snapped his spine with one hand, broad as he was. But he had the badge and he knew it. I shut my mouth.

Fidelia asked gently, "Is there any reason for all this argument? Is this a police station or a debating society?"

He stared at her with the rancor of the poor man looking at money. "I asked you a question when you came in, Mrs. Richards. You haven't answered."

"I answered," she said. "Not with words, but I shook my head. I'm not ready to admit I lied. I'm not ready to even admit I'm Mrs. Richards—not until my attorney advises me to."

"Your attorney is not here, Mrs. Richards."

"He will be," she said. "I phoned him."

Loepke looked surprised and then glared at Mel Braun.

Mel said, "She asked me to wait outside until she changed her shoes."

Loepke started to say something and then the phone on his desk rang. He picked it up. He said, "Sergeant Loepke." A pause. "Oh, yes, sir." A pause. "Of course, sir." A frown. "Nothing like that, sir. It's an unfair charge." A pause. "Immediately, sir. The back corridor."

He replaced the phone on its cradle and looked at Mel. He said, "That was the Mayor. He wants us to meet him in the Chief's office, right now."

We all stood up. Loepke came around from behind his desk to lead the way. I was grinning.

He stopped directly in front of me. "What's funny, Puma?"

I said, "The naivete of a grown man who doesn't realize that you don't have to fight city hall if you can buy it."

42

His eyes were murderous and his voice a growl. "You stinking, lousy dago!"

I'm usually thick-skinned, but not about that word. The redness took over my mind and my right hand swung automatically toward the jut of his jaw.

I caught him above the button but with enough force to slam him into the wall. Dust flew and his hand went sliding in under his jacket and nausea welled in me as I realized he was unbalanced enough at the moment to use a gun.

Then Mel Braun was between us, holding onto Loepke's gun hand, and Mel's voice was shrilly urgent. "Sergeant, for Christ's sake, get hold of yourself. Don't—"

Loepke took a deep breath and his hand came out without the gun in it. He said hoarsely, "Lock him up. I don't give a damn what the Mayor or the Chief think about it. Lock him up. Right now! Hear?"

"I will, I will," Mel said soothingly. "He struck you. I was a witness to that."

"Were you a witness to what he called me, Mel?" I asked.

Braun didn't answer. He said, "This way, Puma. Let's go."

I knew the way. I had been there before.

They put me into a cell next to a vomiting drunk, a drunk who had nothing left to vomit but kept hoping he'd bring up *something*. I was still rattled by the violence of the office incident and my own nausea wasn't helped by the horrible sounds from my neighbor.

I sat on the steel bunk and tried to calm down. I can play it cool for only so long and then my Italian temper builds to a climax. And usually gets me into trouble.

Fidelia's illustrious attorney had undoubtedly phoned his brother, the Mayor, and the conference now going on had resulted. To a professional police officer like Loepke a situation of that kind was bound to be embarrassing and demeaning. My smile had been cruel and pointless. I had goaded him; the guilt was mine.

The man next door stopped making noises. He sat on his bunk and looked sickly at the concrete floor. Somewhere, a door clanged and a water pipe rattled under

43

pressure. Through the barred window, I could hear the traffic outside. Dust motes sparkled in the ray of light coming through the window.

A few minutes of this made me nervous; I thought of the boys who had years of it behind them and ahead of them. I wondered if that was what kept me narrowly on the right side of the law. I had some of the instincts of the criminal, certainly, though I hated most of the criminals I had met.

I heard footsteps and looked up expectantly, but the turnkey went past and down another corridor. Damn it, how long was this absurd situation going to last?

Perhaps they were waiting for Fidelia's attorney to get here. It wasn't likely the big man would come; he would send one of his lesser associates.

I heard footsteps again. The turnkey was coming back. I went to the steel door. "I'd like to make a phone call," I said. "Would you tell Captain Amos that?"

He nodded, smiled, and went on. Annoyance mounted in me. It would build to resentment and peak to rage if I didn't fight it. I went back to the bunk, sat down and tried to think sweet thoughts.

The drunk began to cry quietly and hopelessly.

Me and my damned muscles! If I weighed a hundred pounds less, I would have avoided a number of bruises and a whole mess of trouble. I didn't take enough lip.

The drunk sniffed, blew his nose, and turned to ask me, "What you in for?"

"Arrogance," I said.

"Me, too," he said. He turned back, his head bowed.

He couldn't have weighed over a hundred and forty; maybe it wasn't my muscles that had made me arrogant. Maybe it was my Italian heritage.

Or maybe the state of the world, a world where hoodlums ran the government through their unions and the citizens crowded Las Vegas to support the hoodlums the unions had overlooked. It was a great time for hoodlums, foreign and domestic.

While a sweet saint like Joe Puma rotted in jail.

Footsteps again, and it was Captain Amos this time. He stood in the corridor and considered me sourly.

"He called me a stinking, lousy dago," I explained.

44

"What am I supposed to do, cringe?"

"No. You're supposed to report him to his superior. That is, if you consider yourself a citizen."

"I am a citizen. I shouldn't have to tell *you* that, Captain."

"Sure, sure," he said wearily. "Well, her lawyer's here now and we can get the great debate started."

The turnkey came and unlocked the door and I went along with Captain Amos to the Chief's office. There were half a dozen people in there: Loepke, the Mayor, the Chief, Braun, Fidelia and a young Ivy League type who was probably an associate of Fidelia's attorney.

Loepke looked at me grimly as I entered; the others viewed me with less interest. Except for Fidelia, who smiled and winked.

"Good afternoon, gentlemen," I said.

Chief Nystrom said, "We can do without any levity, Mr. Puma. Take that chair next to Detective Braun. Captain, that chair next to Sergeant Loepke."

When we were seated, he said, "And now, Mr. Puma, your story."

I shook my head. "I'm sorry, sir, but I don't care to speak unless my attorney is present."

There was a silence. Chief Nystrom's face was composed but his eyes burned dangerously.

I asked, "Has any charge been made? This is all a little too informal for me."

Loepke said, "I can give you two—adulterous conduct and assaulting a police officer." He paused. "And perjury."

The young lawyer said quickly, "Just one moment, Sergeant."

The Mayor raised a hand. "Just one moment, *everybody*," he said. "Let us all remember that our important concern is a murder that took place last night and the only possible perjury we are concerned with at this moment is perjury that might have retarded or interfered with the investigation of that murder."

Loapke asked quietly, "What about the assault, sir?"

It took a lot of guts for Loepke to say that, and I gazed at him admiringly.

The Mayor said stiffly, "We are not concerned with

45

that *at the moment,* Sergeant. First things first." He looked at me. "I understand you've been hired to investigate the murder."

I nodded. "And I'd be glad to give Sergeant Loepke all I've learned so far." I took a breath. "I'm sorry I hit him, but he shouldn't have called me what he did."

Captain Amos said mildly, "If Mr. Puma intends to do any investigating in our town, he will have to work very closely with the Department. He understands that." He looked at me.

I nodded. "Though we can't be sure, of course, that the murder happened in this town. So far as we know now, the last time Brian Delsy was seen alive he was in Venice."

There was another silence. I looked over to see Loepke glowering and Mel Braun staring glumly into space.

The Mayor looked at Loepke uncertainly and then at Captain Amos hopefully. The Captain was the peacemaker here.

Captain Amos said, "I'm sure we're all agreed that Mrs. Richards has been the victim of unfortunate publicity too often. It is not our job to feed a sensational Los Angeles press with further defamatory material. And certainly not at the risk of a lawsuit." He cleared his throat. "Mr. Puma's attack on a police officer was lamentable and unwarranted. Sergeant Loepke used improper language, but that still doesn't excuse Mr. Puma."

They all looked at me, now. I looked at Loepke and Loepke looked off into space.

I said, "What I did was wrong, but I can't guarantee I won't do it again to the next man who calls me that."

The Chief said, "Perhaps Mr. Puma hasn't cooled enough. We'll hold him for a while and decide his fate later. You may go, Mrs. Richards."

My Fidelia, my faithful, shook her head. "I need him."

The Chief looked startled, the Mayor frowned.

The young attorney said, "Mrs. Richards, I think Chief Nystrom has been more than fair in this and I urgently suggest that you accept the——"

"No," she said firmly. "I need Joe Puma. And I should think the Department here would welcome him as an ally. Certainly, you're all familiar with his impressive record?"

46

Hey, what a girl! I stared at her in unadulterated reverence—a discerning, forthright, loyal and delectable doll.

The Chief coughed, the Mayor frowned. Captain Amos said, "I'm well aware of Mr. Puma's qualifications, Mrs. Richards. And I must admit his record is as clean as his trade will permit. However, his license does not give him the right to assault an officer. Mr. Puma combines an awesome physique with an atrocious temper and his arrogance is infamous."

It wasn't a bad analysis; this Captain Aaron Amos was sharp.

Another long silence and Loepke finally broke it. "I guess it's fair to say both Puma and I were out of line. I'm willing to forget it if everybody else is."

The Mayor beamed, the Chief looked relieved. Fidelia smiled, her lawyer sighed, Mel Braun frowned and Loepke continued to glower.

"I apologize, Sergeant," I said. "I goaded you at a bad time. The whole thing was really my fault."

The Chief asked, "A bad time? What does that mean, Mr. Puma?"

"In a world run by hoodlums," I said, "the Sergeant is old-fashioned enough to try to be honest. I guess the rest of us know that's impossible, today."

The Mayor said stiffly, "Speak for yourself, sir. I've managed it."

Captain Amos said, "Mr. Puma is both physically and orally arrogant. And his standards of alleged honesty are perhaps more distorted than ours. Well, sir, we can use him, despite that."

That Amos, he was a one.

There was a sense of relaxed tension throughout the room now. The Mayor rose and said, "Do you see what an open discussion can do? That's the American way."

He smiled at all of us and went out to the imagined sound of a Marine band.

The Chief rose, said, "Captain, you will brief Mr. Puma and he'll report to you if he stays on this case."

Amos nodded and the Chief left the room. Loepke and Braun left without comment. Fidelia said, "We'll need a ride back, Captain."

Her attorney said, "My car's here. I can drop both

47

you and Mr. Puma off, Fidelia."

"Mr. Puma will be out soon," Amos told them. "Come with me, Joe."

I went with him to an office he shared with Lieutenant Carlson and there I gave him the résumé of my day's interviews. He took down what seemed pertinent in a self-invented shorthand he used.

When I had finished, he looked up and smiled. "Okay, these are the facts. What's your hunch?"

"You don't work on hunches, Captain."

"I respect yours," he said.

"I think this Robert Tampett should be sweated. I wouldn't tag him as a murderer; he's too cute for that. But he sure as hell knows more than he told me."

"We'll lean on him," he said. "And Joe, watch your mouth around Sergeant Loepke. That's a warning."

I nodded.

He smiled. "Adulterous conduct. What a mild phrase to use about a satyr. So long. Keep in touch night and day."

I waved good-bye and went out into the sun again. In her attorney's car, my Fidelia was waiting for me with a big smile. I certainly picked some dandies.

Chapter Six

It had been a full day, starting with my discovery of Delsy's body this morning. I was emotionally and physically fatigued. And I was hungry.

At the cottage, Fidelia asked, "Why don't we have dinner together someplace? You can put it on the expense account and I can owe you."

"Fine," I said. "But I have to go to the office to check the mail and my answering service. And I need a clean shirt and like that." I computed it in my mind. "How about six-thirty?" It was now five o'clock.

She shook her head. "I want to go along. I don't want to be alone, Joe."

So she went along. In Westwood, she waited in the car

48

while I managed a quick shave, shower and change in my apartment. In Beverly Hills, she came up to my office with me.

There was a check and two bills in my mail, the check bigger than the total of the bills. So that was all right. My phone answering service reported that a Lou Serano had phoned me, but left no number to call.

Lou Serano was the hoodlum who had sat with Bob Tampett in the booth at Eddie's last night. None of the various local phone books helped me with him, nor could "Information." I had a feeling he would call again.

In and around Beverly Hills there are a number of fine restaurants, but Fidelia said, "Why don't we go to Eddie's? His steaks are pretty good. And we can listen to Pete's piano."

"With Pete off the soup," I asked, "will he still be at Eddie's?"

She nodded. "His contract runs until the end of the week and he *always* honors a contract." She sighed. "I wonder how long he'll stay on the wagon."

"Was the booze the big item in your breakup?" I asked her.

She shrugged. "It could have been. He's one of those drunks who hates you unless you drink along with him. God, the things he'd call me when I wouldn't!"

I asked, "If he ever got on the wagon permanently, would you go back to him?"

She shook her head. "We can't go back." She looked up at me wistfully. "We can't ever go back, can we?"

"Never," I agreed. "That's what finally kills us, one way or another. Let's go."

We went down the steps and into the early evening sun. She stood on the curb and looked at my dusty Plymouth and said, "You could wash it, at least. Why do you have to be the professional poor man?"

"It helps me maintain my sanity," I explained. "Let's go! I'm hungry."

She was silent for most of the trip. *Some* thoughts she must have been thinking. Because when we were almost to Eddie's, she asked quietly, "Joe, you didn't kill Brian, did you?"

"Of course not," I said. "What a hell of a question!"

49

"Don't be shocked," she said. "You know *anyone* can kill. You must have realized that, by now."

"It's not true," I said. "I've known people who can't even kill flies or spiders or ants. This morning, I was suspicious of you. But I know now, Fidelia, you're another person who can't kill."

"Nothing but myself," she said. "Right?"

I didn't answer. She had shown very little self-pity and I didn't mean to encourage any smidgin that broke through.

At Eddie's, Pete Richards hadn't arrived. He didn't come on until later. A few customers were eating steaks, the only entree on the non-existent menu. We ordered New York cuts. And beer.

Eddie was behind the bar and I had some questions to ask him, but it didn't seem like the time. He had greeted Fidelia courteously when we came in but his eyes had just slid over me with no sign of recognition. The slob was sulking.

The steaks were better than I'd expected. The beer was excellent, tap beer, and cool. The back door was open and the smell of the sea drifted in. Some of the day's tensions left me as I sat back and enjoyed the beer.

The customers in view looked normal enough; perhaps last night's tragedy had frightened off Brian's unfortunate companions. The police would be giving this bar special attention for a few days.

Pete Richards came in, looking weary but sober, and waved at us before going over to the piano.

His music didn't seem as alien to my taste tonight. There still seemed to be less melody than harmony, but a thread of melody began to persist in my mind. I can't say honestly that I followed it, but I enjoyed it.

After his first half-hour session, he came over to our booth, bringing a cup of coffee along. He sat down next to me and looked inquiringly at Fidelia.

"Beautiful," she said. "You get better every day. That last—that was brand new, wasn't it?"

He nodded.

"What are you calling it?" she asked.

" 'Requiem for a Lost Lady'." He smiled. "Nothing personal, Fidelia." His eyes went past her toward the door. Then he looked quickly at me. "Here's the man I mentioned this afternoon, coming in now."

I turned to see a tall, skinny, smooth and swarthy gent coming through the doorway. His shoulders were narrow, his chest cavernous, his tailoring straight from the Strip. His big, brown eyes considered me impersonally before shifting to Pete. He waved at Pete and headed our way.

"Serano?" I guessed quietly. "Lou Serano?"

"Right," Pete said. "Hell, he's coming over!"

He came over and smiled down at us. "Hello, kiddies. You look cozy."

Fidelia said, "Hello, Lou," and sipped her beer.

Serano smiled at Pete. "I missed the first session, huh?" Pete nodded.

Serano looked at me. "And who's the new face?"

"My name," I said, "is J. Edgar Hoover. Start running, punk."

Fidelia looked startled, Pete Richards embarrassed. I had made an ass of myself again, but I couldn't help it. I hated him. The hair on my neck had started to bristle as soon as I had seen him.

A silence. Serano exhaled heavily and stared at me with no fear I could notice. "What's your beef, big boy?"

"I hate hoodlums," I explained. "I'm sorry, but that's the way it's always been. You may not even be a hoodlum, but you look like one. I'm getting sick. Go away."

"I think I know you," he said thoughtfully.

"Then run," I said. "Go, man."

"You've a reputation for being tough," he persisted. "How tough, Puma?"

I looked up into his quiet brown eyes. "Tough enough to play it alone. Tough enough so that I never needed the help of a mob." I started to get up.

But Pete Richards was on the open side of me, and he put a hand on my arm. "Easy, now, Joe. No trouble, please."

Serano said, "Don't worry, there won't be any. I'm not a mug, a bar-fighter." He threw his thin shoulders back and met my glare steadily. "I've a feeling you're not long for this world, Puma."

He gave us his well-tailored back and went to the bar.

51

I sat down again and met Fidelia's wondering gaze.

"I'm sorry," I said. "They make me sick."

"Maybe you see yourself in them," she said quietly.

I said nothing.

"He might have been carrying a gun," she pointed out.

"He'd have eaten it," I answered.

Pete Richards chuckled. "You've been watching those westerns on TV, Joe. Be reasonable, man; you can't lick the world."

"I can die trying," I told him. "Let's have another beer." I signaled the waiter.

"Coffee for me," Richards said.

"I want to go," Fidelia said. "I want to drive along the ocean and smell the salt air. I want to get out of here."

When the waiter came, I paid the check. and we went out. On the sidewalk Fidelia took a deep breath of the sea air. "People!" she said. "People, ugh!"

"It's been a bad day for people," I said. "We got all the wrong ones in a bunch."

She nodded silently. Then she looked up at me. "Joe, I don't want to drive along the beach. I want to go home. I'm bushed. I want to be alone. No offense?"

"Of course not. Why should I take offense?"

She didn't answer. She walked over to the car and I held the door for her. She got in and I closed the door and went around to get behind the wheel.

This lassitude had come over her suddenly, I thought, but she had a reputation as a moody girl. Had something happened back at Eddie's that I hadn't noticed, something to change her mood abruptly?

She didn't say a word on the trip to the cottage. There, I walked to the door with her and she patted my cheek, said good night and started to go in.

"Fidelia," I asked, "are you all right?"

"I will be," she answered. "A good night's sleep is all I need. Don't be upset, now; it's just my weariness."

"Okay. Good night."

She smiled and closed the door.

I had a hunch that it would be smart to park somewhere out of sight and watch the cottage, but she was my client. I drove away.

52

Shaved, showered and wearing a clean shirt, and it was only nine o'clock. It would be a waste to go home. I went back to Eddie's.

Lou Serano was still there, now sitting in the booth we had deserted. He was eating a steak and he wasn't alone. Bob Tampett was having a steak too, sitting across from Serano.

Serano was facing the door and he said something to Tampett when he saw me. Tampett turned, glanced contemptuously at me, and went back to his steak. Serano smiled.

I went to the bar and ordered a bourbon and water.

Eddie's face was stiff and he didn't look at me as he served it.

I asked, "Got any kids, Eddie?"

He looked at me coolly. "Two. A boy and a girl. Both in high school."

"Addicted to narcotics?" I asked.

He stood perfectly still. "Watch your big mouth."

I said, "That's Lou Serano sitting in that booth with Tampett. If Lou had his way, *all* the high school kids would be on the needle."

Eddie said nothing, glaring at me.

"But you hate *me*, not *him*," I said. "That's what bugs me."

He said quietly, "How many of you private eyes are ex-cons? You think you're the first one I ever met?"

"I hold a license," I explained, "from the state. So I'm clear. I'll grant you some of the licensed boys hire ex-cons for tough help, but I'm a one-man agency. You can ask any police officer over at the Venice Station about me, Eddie."

"So you're clean," he said. "That makes us buddies?"

"I'm clean and I hate hoodlums. That should make me a brother to any man with kids in high school. Or am I getting too profound for you?"

"You're sure a mouthy bastard," he said. He wiped the bar, looked over at the booth and back at me. "What do you want from me?"

"Everything that went on here after Mrs. Richards and I left last night."

53

"I bounced Delsy. Then Tampett went back to that booth and in a couple minutes Serano came in. He went over and sat with Tampett and they yacked. Richards joined them later, for about twenty minutes, between sessions."

"Richards?" I asked. "This afternoon he had a hard time remembering if Tampett had company."

Eddie shrugged. "He was loaded. That figures. This Pete Richards, he'll all right, Puma. I don't understand his music, but he's on the up and up."

"I'd like to think so, too," I admitted. "But that's a bad investigative attitude."

At my elbow, someone asked, "Calmed down, now?" I turned to face Lou Serano.

"I phoned you this morning," he said. "Didn't you get the message?"

I nodded. "But you're not in the book. I couldn't call back."

"I see," he said. "But when I walked in here tonight, you start flexing your muscles. Why?"

"It had been a bad day," I explained. "I'd been jailed and lectured and threatened. A citizen like me. And then I sit here in my cheap suit and in you walk with that Strip tailoring, looking like you own the world. Are you a citizen, Lou?"

"Hell, yes. I pay my taxes. That doesn't look like a cheap suit, Puma."

"I got it on sale," I explained. "What's on your mind?"

"A talk," he said. "Do you want to come over to the booth?"

I looked at the booth. Tampett had left. I walked over there with Serano and sat down.

With operators like Serano, it's hard to tell where sincerity leaves off and the pitch begins. He sure as hell looked serious and sincere as he gave me the "word."

He has a Vegas friend, he told me, a pretty big man who had a piece of one of the better sucker traps, a man who had reason to admire Fidelia Sherwood Richards.

"Do you want to name the man?" I asked.

"No. But believe me, Puma, he's first class."

Nobody in Vegas was first class in my book, but he

54

wasn't quoting from my book. "Go on," I said.

"This gent's got a wife, one he's had for eight years, and she got a little mixed up a couple years back and she went to this Dr. Foy. The damned quack almost put her in the bughouse for good. For *life*. It took the best psychiatrist in this town two years to cure her of Dr. Foy. You follow me?"

"I think so. But why come to me? Why don't you tell this to Mrs. Richards?"

"Because, according to my friend, it could put her over the edge. The way these quacks work, she's probably completely dependent on him, now. That's the way they operate. In Fidelia's case, he could lead her by the nose right up to the altar. The quack's not married, you know."

"All right. I'll repeat my question—why come to me?"

"Because, right now, you're it."

I stared at him.

"Don't get hot," he said. "I mean, right now, she trusts you. She *depends* on you, see? And maybe you can wean her from this Dr. Foy. It takes time and patience."

"Time I won't have," I said. "I'm only a temporary employee."

He smiled. "That's your only relationship, huh—employer-employee?"

I stared at him. "What else?"

He shook his head. "All right. All right! You're a hard man to talk sense to, Puma."

"Sit where I'm sitting," I told him. "Pretend you're Puma, and a notorious pusher tries to sell you the pitch that he's such a great humanitarian he's worried about the future of poor little Fidelia Sherwood. There's not a dime in it for the pusher, you understand—just his big compassionate heart."

He sat erectly in the booth and his narrow shoulders went back defiantly. "I'm not a *notorious* pusher. I was a guy who was *on* it. And to keep me going, while I was on it, I had to push it. Where else would I get the dough *that* costs? I broke the habit. So much for that."

"And now you're going into social work?" I asked.

"No, not by a damned sight. But this boy in Vegas asked me to do him a favor, because he knew I knew

Fidelia. And you do boys like that favors, it might not mean an immediate dime, but it sure as hell isn't going to hurt my career, huh?"

"And what's your career?" I asked.

"A fast buck," he said. "What's yours?"

He could be telling the truth. Even if it was the first time in his life, he could be telling the truth. I said, "I suppose you briefed yourself on Dr. Arnold Foy?"

"Open your ears and sit back," he said.

Chapter Seven

How I slept that night. . . . Without dreams, like falling into oblivion, like dying. I wakened to an overcast morning, damp and smoggy.

I read the *Times* with my coffee. In its thorough way, the *Times* had all the details of the Brian Delsy murder, though there was nothing in the account I didn't know. The Fidelia-Puma bit that followed the murder yesterday afternoon was absent from the *Times,* so Loepke had obviously not confided in the reporters he had threatened us with.

My phone rang as I was shaving; it was Fidelia.

"When are you coming over?" she asked.

"Not until I have something to report," I answered. "You hired me as an investigator, not a bodyguard."

A silence, and then, "Are you angry about something? About last night?"

"Of course not," I said gently. I took a breath. "Fidelia, you are much more self-sufficient than you realize. You need my abilities temporarily, but you don't need *me* any more than you need anyone else. Hasn't Foy told you that?"

"Not quite as bluntly," she answered. "Joe, I will see you today, some time, won't I?"

"If you really need me," I said, "I can be there in fifteen minutes. If you don't, I'll drop in this afternoon."

A long pause. And then, "About three-thirty this afternoon?"

"I'll be there," I promised.

I hung up reflecting that she had two rocks now, Foy and Puma. And both of them were hired friends. And was Foy any kind of friend?

I went out and headed for Wilshire. . . .

The Sunset College of Clinical Psychology advertised in various magazines, some newspapers and occasionally by direct mail. I had never heard the college advertise on the radio or TV and could guess why. I would hate to trust an announcer with a tongue twister like Sunset College of Clinical Psychology.

It occupied a suite of offices on the second floor of a new building near Fairfax. The receptionist in the waiting room had glossy black hair piled high on her head, a dusky complexion, and an intriguing cleavage.

I told her my name was Temple Hawkins Reeve and I was interested in their courses.

She told me the chancellor, Dr. Alecont, would see me in a few minutes, and would I please wait?

I waited in a foam-cushioned Danish-modern chair and looked around. There were some magazines on the table next to me, and I checked through them. *Time, Life* and the *A.M.A. Journal.* Now there was a touch, that last. There is probably no law that prevents the *A.M.A. Journal* from being found anywhere, and it did add a touch of authenticity for the gullible.

And I was sure that Dr. Alecont catered to a widely different pair of groups. One would be the sharks and the other the gullible.

I intended to impersonate a shark.

In a few minutes, the stacked brunette rose from behind her burnished walnut desk and went quietly to a door that opened off a small corridor.

She went through it, closing it behind her. Less than a minute after that she returned and told me Dr. Alecont would see me now.

I went into a walnut-paneled office, furnished in gray and dusty yellow, with walnut-framed diplomas on the walls. I had heard of none of the schools represented except for the Sunset College of Clinical Psychology, where *Doctor* Alecont had earned his doctorate.

57

He was tall and dark, with a goatee and pince-nez—
quite an authentic reproduction of a society doctor in
an old Universal or Columbia picture.

"Good morning, Mr. Reeve," he said sonorously.
"Won't you be seated?"

I sat in the chair on the sucker's side of his desk and
he sat down again and smiled at me. "A local resident,
Mr. Reeve?"

"Long Beach," I said. "I was in oil down there, and
real estate. And I dabbled in second mortgages, of course."

"Of course," he said warmly. "And now?"

"Well," I said, "it occurred to me I've spent a lot of
time in the wrong professions."

"Oh?" he said.

"I've always been interested in psychology, and you
know something, Doctor?"

He smiled encouragingly. "What?"

"People confide in me. At parties and on busses, they
tell me the damnedest things?"

"Busses?" he asked, frowning. If I had said "planes"
or "trains," I'll bet he wouldn't have frowned.

"Sure," I went on. "Busses. Perfect strangers."

"Hmmmm," he said thoughtfully. "You mentioned oil
and real estate. You were, or are, a speculator, Mr.
Reeve?"

I smiled and shook my head. "A promoter, Dr. Alecont.
I—don't like to operate on my own money."

His answering smile was doubtful. "And the second-
trust deeds?"

"I had a small office," I explained, "and acted as broker for second-trust deeds."

"I see," he said, and studied me. He had his picture
of me now, a smalltime grifter, assets unknown. He
smiled. "And you feel that psychology is your forte?"

"I sure do, Doctor. I always had a bent for getting
people to talk and I've helped a lot of them. Free, of
course."

"Of course," he said. "What's your educational background, Mr. Reeve?"

"I had a year and a half at Stanton Teacher's College."
I looked at him candidly. "I had some psychology there."

"That will help," he said thoughtfully. "We offer three

58

degrees here, Mr. Reeve—bachelor, master and doctor. The length of study for any of the degrees would be determined by your own aptitude and application, of course."

"Of course," I said. He had me doing it, now. "And the fees?"

"The initial tuition," he said, "is two hundred dollars. That includes the basic texts. Further fees are based on the number of examinations you will require to earn your desired degree. You seem like a highly intelligent man, Mr. Reeve, and I'm sure you'll have no trouble getting through our examinations."

He couldn't have made it clearer if he'd winked. I felt like a star quarterback at a football college.

I hesitated, studying the top of his desk.

"Is something troubling you, Mr. Reeve?" he asked gently.

I looked up sheepishly. "Well, yes. Damn it, Dr. Alecont, I feel qualified *right now*. I mean, the way people tell me things and the way I helped them, I'll bet I'm as good as most of the psychologists I see practicing around Long Beach."

"It's entirely possible," he admitted. "Then why did you come to us, Mr. Reeve?"

I held my breath, so it would look like I was blushing. I said quietly, "Well, that diploma— I mean, a man, a professional man, should have *something* hanging on his wall, something that makes his customers—I mean his patients—realize he's, well, qualified, if you get me."

"I understand," he said softly, "and there are provisions for that. "Any time you can pass the examinations that lead to a doctorate here, you will be able to achieve it after payment of the proper fees. You have to understand, Mr. Reeve, that though we are not as traditionally strict as the larger schools, we must maintain standards."

I nodded. "Naturally. I understand that. If I passed these exams, how much would the fees be?"

"Five hundred dollars," he said firmly, studying me for a reaction.

"Cash?" I asked. "In advance?"

"Not necessarily. We are willing to work out agreeable financial arrangements for the convenience of any student

59

who is worthy of it."

"Gosh," I said, "I don't know. Five hundred dollars, huh? And I call myself Dr. Temple Hawkins Reeve?"

He smiled benignly. "A very impressive title, Mr. Reeve."

"Five hundred dollars," I said musingly. "I wonder if I could pass the exams?"

"We have a comprehensive text," he said, "which you will read before you take the examination for the doctorate. I guarantee you will pass the examination after reading that text." He smiled. "No student has *ever* failed the examination after reading that text."

"Gosh," I said. "Five hundred dollars."

He paused, frowning. Then, "We have another arrangement, Mr. Reeve. You pay us three hundred now and two hundred, plus interest, out of your earnings, once you have set up your practice."

"That sounds more like my dish of tea," I said. "That sounds real fair, Dr. Alecont." I stood up. "I'll sure think that over. There's another school on Santa Monica Boulevard I wanted to check before deciding, but I don't mind telling you this course of yours sounds very fine."

"Another school?" he asked worriedly. "Are you referring to the Stacy Studio of Psychic Research?"

"That's the one," I agreed. "I know psychic research isn't psychology, not today, maybe, but today's superstition is tomorrow's science and vice versa, right, Dr. Alecont?"

"Never," he said rigidly. "If you don't mind a frank professional opinion, Mr. Reeve, the Stacy Studio is highly suspect. And they've had a lot of trouble with the Better Business Bureau only recently. A degree from that place is—is *meaningless!*"

"They've got a real impressive diploma," I argued.

"Impressive?" he asked heatedly, his goatee quivering. He pointed toward his on the wall. "Take a good look at that one, Mr. Reeve, and *then* tell me the Stacy diploma is impressive. Take a long look."

I went over to examine it. It was a beauty, all right. A rich parchment with embossed printing and a shining, embossed gold seal over twin baby-blue ribbons. It was a sweetheart. It made U.C.L.A. look like a cow college.

"Five hundred dollars," I said musingly.

"All right," he said impatiently, "all right! I guess we're both men of the world. Two hundred dollars, no examination, and you walk out of this office as Dr. Temple Hawkins Reeve. I guess I know a qualified man when I see one."

I shrugged, looking thoughtful.

"Those quacks at the Stacy Studio will never match that," he assured me. "And think of the prestige. We're not going to *haggle*, are we, Mr. Reeve?"

"We're not even going to do business," I said quietly.

He stared at me, his eyes wary. His mouth opened, and closed.

"I'm a patient of Dr. Arnold Foy's," I said. "I only dropped in to assure myself of his qualifications."

His mouth opened again. "You—you— Get out of here! I'll have the police—"

"Relax," I said. "I'm not after you. I just wanted to see if the twelve hundred dollars I spent with Dr. Foy were well spent. I've seen enough. Good day to you, Doctor."

"Get out, you grifter," he said.

In the waiting room, the mammarial brunette looked up anxiously. The Doctor's voice had been strident.

"Terrible disposition, hasn't he?" I asked her. "I hope you're well paid."

"He's a fine man," she said frigidly. "A scholar and a gentleman."

"And a quack," I added. "What an unusual combination. Well, it's the Stacy Studio for me!" That was my exit line.

Outside, the sun was trying to break through the overcast but not making it. The smog made my eyes sting.

Doctor Arnold Foy's degree had come from this "school" I had just left. Was it only in Los Angeles that a man like Foy could attract patients at the Sherwood level? He had helped her, she had claimed. How? If he had helped her, she hadn't needed help.

Dr. Foy had seemed too confident, too sure, to be trusted. I knew nothing of the field, but this I knew: any man who was *sure* of anything today, including the multiplication table, was either a fool or a fraud. And Dr.

Foy had given no indication of being a fool.

Could I bring to Fidelia this story of Sunset College? Not yet. It would be taking away her rock. I headed for Brentwood.

It was an older house, small and faintly Spanish. The front yard was all crushed rock and cacti, yucca, jade plant and stratified boulders, streaked in black. An enormous bird of paradise tree shaded the small front patio. A minimum upkeep yard.

The woman who answered to my ring had faded blue eyes and bleached hair, the roots brown. She was wearing shorts and a T shirt and thong sandals. She was atractively sun-browned, but her face was taut and her breasts weren't.

"Well?" she asked.

"Mrs. Foy?" I asked.

"Right. So?"

"My name is Joseph Puma," I said. "I'm a private investigator."

"Oh, Jesus!" she said. "What's he dreamed up now? Don't tell me he's going to make me trouble again?"

"If you mean your former husband," I answered, "he didn't send me. I came here to ask about him."

Relief softened her tense face and she smiled wryly. "You came to the right place, Sherlock. Come in, come in."

I entered a small hall and from there into a living room furnished with crude and dusty mission furniture, dark and heavy. The ashtrays were all filled with cigarettes; in the dining room the dishes on the table indicated it hadn't been cleared for at least three meals.

"You'll have to excuse the house," she said. "It takes me four cups of coffee to stoke up enough energy to attack it. Sit down wherever it's comfortable for you."

I sat in a heavy, wooden chair with leather seat. "Why did you think your ex-husband had sent me?" I asked.

"Why not? Would you like a cup of coffee? The place might give you the wrong idea; I make damned good coffee. Even Arnie admits that."

"I'd like a cup, thank you."

She went into the kitchen and I looked around. Disorderly, yes, but comfortable, for some reason. As she was.

She brought me back a cup of coffee and it was fine. She took hers to a worn, sagging couch and sat down with her legs curled under her.

I asked again, "Why did you think your ex-husband had sent me?"

"Twice he's tried to have me committed to some quack rest home and alcoholic's haven he has an interest in. That was before we were divorced. Since then, I've made a scene in his office a couple of times. I suppose that's bad for business and I have a hunch he'll be making a move one of these days."

"A move?" I asked. "Certainly you don't expect him to resort to physical action?"

"He's hit me. He's a violent man when things don't go his way. And let me tell you, they didn't go his way for a long time."

"How long has he been a psychologist?" I asked.

She wrinkled her forehead. "Let's see. It'll be five years next month. Before that, he had this cult out in the hills above Malibu. That one didn't pan out. Cults don't pay unless you got a real gimmick, and he didn't."

"And before that?" I prompted her.

"Before that, he was a chauffeur," she told me, "for a wealthy Pasadena family I don't want to name. He knocked up the daughter and took a settlement instead of the wedding ceremony. He lost all that money in the cult."

"And before that?"

"I didn't know him before that," she said. "I met him at the cult. From what one of his old friends has told me, I guess he was a beach bum. Why the biography bit, Hawkshaw?"

"Because I wondered where he got his education," I said.

"He never had any, or nothing to amount to anything. He learned about clothes from that Pasadena family and he learned about women at the cult. I was one of them."

"He's very successful," I said. "Don't you think he should have more education than he has to treat patients

63

who could conceivably be seriously ill?"

"Hell, yes," she said. "But I didn't set the standards for psychologists in this crummy state. Write your assemblyman, Buster."

I asked her quietly, "Do you know Fidelia Sherwood?".

"I've seen her name in the papers," she said. "Why?"

"She's one of your husband's patients."

"God help her!" She stretched her legs out and kicked off the thong sandles. "Who told you about me? I'm not in the book."

"A man I met last night."

"Tampett, maybe?" she asked. "No, he wouldn't sell Arnie out."

"Sell him out? You mean Tampett works for Dr. Foy?"

She nodded. "You got a cigarette?"

I gave her one and held a light for her. I came back to settle in the heavy chair again and she blew smoke toward the center of the room.

"Tampett," she said, "is a cute one. I don't know if he was ever queer or is now, but he knows all the pansies and hangs around their favorite joints. And the ones that have the money and the inclination to change——why, he steers them to Arnie and between Arnie and Bob the poor sucker really gets milked."

I said softly, "The man who was killed night before last, that Brian Delsy, he was a patient of Foy's. And the last man to see him alive, so far as we know now, was Robert Tampett."

She stared at me and the hand holding the cigarette trembled. "Murder?" she said hoarsely. "You think Arnie——?"

I shrugged. "Nobody knows anything yet. Do you think Dr. Foy is capable of committing murder?"

"Hell, yes! He's capable of anything." She took a deep breath and stared at her trembling hands. "Cripes, I need a drink." She looked up helplessly. "Get it for me, will you? On the drainboard in the kitchen. Pour me a real jolt, will you?"

I started to protest, but then realized it was a bad time for a lecture on the evils of alcoholism. I went to the kitchen, poured her a third of a tumbler of the super-

64

market bourbon I found there, and brought it back to her.

She swallowed half of it in the first gulp. She sniffed, brushed back her hair with her wrist, and looked up at me piteously.

"I doubt if it was Foy," I reassured her. "What reason would he have?"

She sniffed again. "Who knows? Who knows what goes on in that conniving mind of *his*?"

"One thing that goes on is self-preservation," I said. "We can bank on that as the prime urge in Dr. Arnold Foy. And murder is an idiot's act."

"You don't know his temper," she said hoarsely. "The things he's called me, and the times he's struck me. Oh, nobody knows that bastard like I do."

"He'll be checked," I assured her. "I'll personally see to that. Are you going to be all right?"

She nodded. "I'll be all right. I'm not an alcoholic, you know. A compulsive drinker, but not an alcoholic."

She and Pete Richards, the same distinction. And how many million others? I thanked her for what she had told me and went out again through the minimum-upkeep front yard to the street.

My car was parked about a half-block away, the only available space when I had arrived. I was walking toward it when I saw the ebony Cadillac convertible moving slowly, the driver looking for a place to park.

I turned to watch it slide into a space in front of Mrs. Foy's house. I waited until the driver got out.

It was Lou Serano.

Chapter Eight

He saw me standing there, and waved. I went back.

"I don't think it's a good time to talk with her," I told him. "That's what you're here for, I suppose?"

He nodded. "I heard a real gone rumour this morning. I heard this Tampett was a shill for Foy, steering the swishes to him."

"Mrs. Foy just told me that. Is that all you wanted to ask her?"

"That's all." He studied me doubtfully. "What's bugging you now?"

"You and Tampett," I answered. "Buddies. How come you didn't know all along he was working for Foy?"

"What am I, the F.B.I.? If I knew, why would I come out here to ask?"

"Maybe you came here for another reason," I said.

His face tightened. "Puma, you don't like me. And you got muscles, so there's nothing I can do about that. But stop and think, if you've got anything to think with. Who steered you onto Mrs. Foy? And that phoney college? That makes me a friend of Foy's or one of his shills? When I started to investigate Foy, Tampett approached me. But he was never any kind of buddy."

It made sense. I said, "I apologize—for now. See you around, Lou."

He went back to his car and I went back to mine. I drove directly to the Santa Monica Police Headquarters.

There, I caught Captain Aaron Amos just as he was ready to go to lunch. I asked him if they'd picked up Tampett.

He shook his head. "Can't seem to find him at home. Got anything new on him?"

I told him what Mrs. Foy had told me.

He frowned. "That ties in Dr. Foy. And he's outside my jurisdiction."

"He's not outside mine, Captain. I'll keep you posted on *him*."

"You make it sound personal," he said.

I said nothing.

"All right," he dismissed me, "we'll pick Tampett up eventually. And I'll let Loepke work on him; that should crack him. Thanks, Joe."

It was past noon now, and I was hungry. I drove over to the Avalon Beach, thinking of Robert Tampett. He had been a friend of Brian Delsy's and Pete Richards' and Fidelia's. He had seemed to be a confidante of Lou Serano. Where was he now?

Fidelia was wearing shorts and a T shirt and she did much better by the combination than Mrs. Foy did.

66

"You told me three-thirty," she teased. "You couldn't stay away, could you?"

"I got hungry," I explained.

She smiled.

"For food," I added. "I thought we could have lunch together."

She pointed to the phone. "Order us a pair of Martinis. I have the menus here."

We drank the Martinis and then they brought our lunch in a tricky cart that kept everything hot.

She asked me, over the lamb chops, where I had spent my morning. I couldn't tell her I'd been checking Foy's college and Foy's ex-wife. Not until I knew how dependent she was on him. .

So I said, "I've been checking out this Tampett. He seems to have disappeared."

There was a silence, and then she said, "I wasn't tired last night. I was angry, Joe. The way you blew up at Lou Serano— And then I remembered how you put the top of your head into poor Brian's face, that night at the bar. And yesterday, when you struck Sergeant Loepke— There's a frightening well of violence in you, isn't there?"

I nodded. "I try to control it. I'm better than I used to be. As a kid, I was much worse; a clawing tiger."

Silence again. She finished her chops and buttered a roll.

I asked, "If it isn't personal, what was in that letter you got from Willis Morley?"

"Some advice," she said. "Some personal advice."

"You don't want to tell me what it was?"

She bit into the roll and shook her head.

"Trust me," I said. "Believe in me. I'm on your side."

She swallowed. "All right. God knows where he heard it, but he warned me against Foy. He said if I needed that kind of help, I should go to an MD, to a psychiatrist. He said Dr. Foy could put me into a state of mind where my estate would be held in trust indefinitely."

"He wasn't lying."

Her chin lifted. "That's why I didn't want to tell you, because I knew you'd agree with him. Joe, I don't want to hear *anything* against Dr. Foy."

67

"Let's talk about Willis, then. I suppose he's worried because if you're judged unfit to inherit the estate, Willis would be out all the money he's advanced you."

"What else?" she asked.

"It's only a guess," I added. "There's a remote possibility that cherubic Willis Morley is as kind and genial as he looks."

She chuckled. "Remote is the word. It's . . . Martian."

"I think I'll drop down there this afternoon, anyway. Maybe Willis knows about somebody besides Dr. Foy."

"I thought we could go to the beach this afternoon," she protested. "It's been such a boring morning!"

"Fidelia, a man is dead. That comes first. Don't you agree?"

Her turquoise eyes looked at me gravely and she nodded. "I was teasing about the beach, anyway. I have an appointment with Dr. Foy this afternoon."

She kept her eyes on my face, as though awaiting a reaction. I tried to look unconcerned, not to show the displeasure I felt.

She had come through a murder and some police rancor; she had witnessed three scenes of Puma semi-violence unscathed. If she was flawed, if she needed psychiatric help, it hadn't been evident to me.

She had an unusual dependence on men, it was true. But I had the same obsessive dependence on women and always considered it normal for a healthy American boy.

"You're thinking about Dr. Foy," she accused me.

I shrugged. "And about Tampett and Sergeant Loepke and Lou Serano and Eddie and Willis Morley and Pete Richards."

"And Mona Greene?" she asked.

I smiled. "Who's Mona Greene?"

She threw a roll at me, and I ducked. She said, "Joe, when this is over, could we take a trip? Could we go to Arrowhead or La Jolla or some place?"

I sighed. "Don't you realize your face is as well known as a movie star's? How could we do a thing like that and stay out of trouble?"

She smiled. "You could be my chauffeur. I could get you a real slick black gabardine uniform and one of those caps with a glossy visor and we'd take a limousine and

68

put on airs and nobody would ever guess."

"I don't like black," I said. "Fidelia, why this compulsion to flout convention?"

"Look who's talking!" she said.

"I'm conventional," I protested, "in many ways. Every way but emotional, I'm highly conventional."

She chuckled. "So am I. I could get you a blue uniform or a gray one."

I finished my coffee and stood up. "We'll think about it. But first things first."

She looked up at me, and, though she tried to play it lightly, there was some wistfulness in her voice. "You don't really like me, do you?"

I held her gaze steadily. "Of course I do. And you know, every person I've met in these last two days shares that emotion. They *all* like Fidelia Sherwood Richards, even sour Eddie."

"Sergeant Loepke doesn't," she answered. "And you called him an honest man. You implied he was about the last honest man in the world."

"Sergeant Loepke," I explained, "is an honest *bitter* man. Because of his job, he has reason to resent the power of wealth, the political power of wealth. So he's not quite normal on that one level. If Sergeant Loepke was the chief of police, he'd love you."

"You're an honest man, and not bitter. Do you love me, Joe?"

"At the moment, yes." I smiled. "But free souls like we are don't love anybody too much very long, do we?"

"You bastard!" she said. "Kiss me and go."

I kissed her and went. The overcast morning had turned into a sunny afternoon without burning away the smog. It got thicker and the traffic murderous as I sent the Plymouth boring into the heart of downtown Los Angeles.

In the shoddy area on Figueroa, the smog seemed to be intensified, and my eyes watered and my sinuses ached as I climbed the steps to Willis Morley's office. Even the odor of new varnish on the handrail couldn't break through this afternoon's smog.

Heirs, Incorporated, still had the dignified *Please Enter* invitation on the door. Willis wasn't wearing the tweed

69

suit; he was more subdued today in salmon gabardine. He looked at me through the open doorway to the waiting room and smiled.

"Come in, Mr. Puma. Didn't you get my check?"

"I haven't been to the office today. That's not why I'm here." I came in and sat in his customer's chair. "Mrs. Richards told me what was in the letter."

He frowned. "And——"

"I wondered what you knew about Foy, Dr. Arnold Foy."

Willis Morley clasped his chubby hands on top of his desk and continued to frown. "Are you here in some—official capacity, Mr. Puma?"

"I'm here looking for an ally, I guess. I have reason to distrust Dr. Foy, myself."

"Oh? And what is your interest in the affairs of Mrs. Richards?"

"Financial," I said, "like yours. She's paying me to investigate the murder of Brian Delsy. Under the assumption that the person who killed him might also be a threat to Mrs. Richards, I'm investigating the people who knew Brian Delsy."

"I didn't know Mr. Delsy."

"You're being evasive, Mr. Morley. I explained to you why I came here."

He unclasped his hands and fiddled with the slide rule again. "Mrs. Richards' attorneys were worried about Dr. Foy's—influence. She won't listen to them, so they appealed to me. They felt Mrs. Richards might listen to me."

I stared at him. "Her attorneys appealed to you? Are you in frequent contact with them?"

"Rather frequent," he said slowly. "After all, I couldn't advance Mrs. Richards the sums I have without some knowledge of her legal claims and the extent of her inheritance. Why should that be surprising, Mr. Puma?"

"Well, I thought, with dignified—— I mean, with probably stuffy lawyers like she'd have——"

He raised a hand. "You assumed men of that stature would not be working with a Figueroa Street loan shark."

"Now, wait, Mr. Morley, I didn't say that."

"You implied it. I'm sure you think of me as a usurer.

70

Some day, when you have the time, figure the interest rates the banks and building-and-loan companies charge. Or the finance companies that specialize in automobile and personal loans. Once the lawyers have dealt with *them*, I appear old-fashioned, Mr. Puma. You see, they don't call it *interest;* the law prevents an overcharge there, though even there the law is too generous. They have fees and commissions and handling charges instead."

I smiled. "But in your old-fashioned way, you think it's really interest."

He said firmly, "Any time you pay rent for money, it's interest, no matter what your bank calls it."

"Well," I said, "now that I realize you're on the side of the angels, Mr. Morley, we can confide in each other. You tell me what you know about Dr. Foy."

He sat quietly, looking like a grim Santa Claus.

"I know some things about him, Mr. Morley. I've talked with his ex-wife and with the chancellor of his so-called college. But perhaps you know something I don't about him?"

Willis Morley shook his head. "The college is all I know about. Except that *Doctor* Foy didn't even graduate from high school."

"Then we're agreed he's not qualified to practice. But what harm can he do Mrs. Richards that would concern you?"

"I explained that," he said mildly, "earlier in our conversation. I was performing a requested service for those in charge of her estate."

"And why are they concerned?"

"Because they are ethical men and she is their client. Because the senior partner of the firm was a very close friend of her father's." Willis looked at me sadly. "Can't you believe, Mr. Puma, that there are people in the world who don't expect to be paid for every good deed?"

"I can believe that, Mr. Morley, because I'm naturally sentimental. But you damned well don't believe it."

He smiled tolerantly and fiddled with the slide rule. "What did you learn from Dr. Foy's wife, Mr. Puma?"

I stood up and looked down at him. "Nothing you've paid me to tell you. We don't seem to be doing each other much good, do we? Don't you believe I'm working for Mrs. Richards?"

"I believe you're working for the money she pays you," he answered, "and honestly earning it. I don't picture you as a knight on a white charger, if that's the illusion you want me to accept."

I shook my head. "I'm disappointed in you, Mr. Morley. And I'm sure Mrs. Richards will be, too."

His bright blue eyes clouded momentarily, and I thought he was about to protest. But all he finally said was, "Good afternoon, Mr. Puma."

What it probably boiled down to was my antipathy for loan sharks and the universal antipathy he shared for private eyes. I nodded a good-bye and went out.

I didn't expect to learn much at my next destination, but there weren't many other places to go. I headed for Dr. Foy's office on Wilshire.

His receptionist was middle-aged and pleasant, a trim gray-haired woman with a soothing voice and a firm chin-line.

I asked her, "Has Mrs. Richards been in yet? I thought I'd meet her here."

She looked perplexed and then studied an appointment book on her desk. She looked up again. "Was she planning to come in? She hasn't an appointment."

"She was planning to come in," I said. "Is Dr. Foy busy now?"

"I can check," she said. "Your name, please?"

I told her my name and she went into his office. She came back in seconds to tell me Dr. Foy was not busy and would see me immediately.

He was sitting behind his desk in there, slim, smooth and handsome. He examined me speculatively as he said, "Good afternoon, Mr. Puma." He waved to a chair.

I nodded to his greeting and sat down. I said, "I'm looking for Robert Tampett. I thought you might know where he is."

He shook his head, still studying me. "I've never heard of him. You've been investigating me, haven't you?"

I nodded.

"Why?"

72

"One of your patients was killed. His body was found next to the cottage of another of your patients. The chief suspect, so far, for the murder is an employee of yours. Add that up, Dr. Foy, and I'm sure you'll realize your question was idiotic."

His face was stone and his eyes glared at me.

I looked over his head, at the fancy diploma with the baby-blue ribbons. I smiled and said, "The Sunset College of Clinical Psychology. Doctor, get off the dignity kick—you're a quack!"

The eyes, too, were stone now, his voice deadly. "Would you be willing to repeat that statement in court?"

I nodded. "Any court you suggest. I'm not one of your frightened widows, Foy. You don't begin to impress me."

He said nothing. On top of his desk, his hands clenched tightly.

I said, "Do you want to go into court and swear you never heard of Robert Tampett?"

He took a deep breath. "Mr. Puma, no matter what you may think of me, I have reason to believe you hold some regard for Mrs. Richards."

I nodded.

"Perhaps," he suggested, "in your layman's ignorance, you assume you have taken my place with her?"

I frowned. "*Your* place? What does that mean?"

"It means she is very dependent on you, perhaps, for some service you are performing. But let me assure you she is *totally* dependent on me." He paused. "For her continued sanity."

I just stared at him.

"Learn for yourself," he said. "Take her to any psychiatrist in this town and get an opinion."

"I intend to," I assured him. "Do you want to tell me where Tampett is now?"

"I have no idea who, or where, he is. But let me repeat, it would be very dangerous to Mrs. Richards for you to destroy my image."

"Hypnosis?" I asked him. "What's your gimmick, Foy?"

"Good-bye," he said coldly.

I stood up. "Something you learned at the cult, maybe? Some drug you've picked up?"

73

"Get out," he said hoarsely. "Get out before I call the police." He reached for the phone, glaring at me.

I picked up the phone and handed it to him. I said, "Call them. I'll wait right here."

He was breathing heavily now and his hands trembled. He replaced the phone shakily on its cradle and stared at the top of his desk. His voice was a strained whisper. "Get out, get out, get out, get out—"

I closed his door quietly behind me. In the outer office, I told his receptionist, "If Mrs. Richards comes in, have her ask the doctor about Robert Tampett. She'd like to be reminded, because she always forgets it when she gets here. Some sort of *block,* you know. I was supposed to remind her, but I can't wait."

The woman nodded. "I'll be sure to tell her, Mr. Puma."

I went to the office to check the mail and my answering service. The calls weren't important; the only important mail was Willis Morley's check. I dropped that off with a deposit slip in the bank's night depository on the way home.

I was getting nowhere and should have been dispirited. But it was always this way before the first break, before the first glimmer of light that might lead to truth. It was always around and around the same deceptive circle, both the innocent and the guilty lying for their own protective reasons, until fright or panic or occasionally even conscience opened a crack to the light.

In my little Westwood cave, I found one cold can of beer in the refrigerator. I took off my shoes and sat on the worn studio couch, nursing the beer and remembering my day, searching for the small and obvious lies that might point a finger.

I was facing the door as I sat there, and I thought I saw the doorknob turn. Right then, I should have moved off that couch. I was only five or six steps from my gun, buried under a pile of shirts in the chest across the room.

But I thought it was an illusion, the weary day and a can of beer on an empty stomach. I didn't move, though I continued to stare at the doorknob.

This time it was no illusion. The knob turned quickly, the door opened and Robert Tampett came in, closing the door behind him. He looked drunk to me.

And he loked dangerous, despite his size. Because there was a revolver in his hand and it was pointed at me.

"You bastard," he said quietly. "You put them on to me, didn't you? You nosed around and dug up the dirt for them."

"For whom?" I asked shakily.

"For the police. You filled them in on me real good, didn't you?"

"Is that the gun that killed Delsy?" I asked him. "Don't tell me you're an amateur and didn't get rid of the gun?"

His smile was twisted and I thought he wavered on his feet. "Why don't you call me 'little man,' like you did before? Maybe I'm not a little man now, huh?"

He sure as hell wasn't, not with that gun in his hand. He was bigger than life.

I licked my lips. "You're drunk, Bob. Don't do anything you'll regret later. That thing could go off, you know, and then you'd really be in the soup. Put it away, and I'll forget you ever had it."

"Forget?" he said. "I didn't come here to scare you; I came here to get you."

"Easy," I said soothingly. "Stop and think. Use your head. Nobody's got a damned thing on you—yet." I hefted the beer can, wondering what luck I'd have if I threw it.

"Don't move," he said. "Don't move and don't whine." His voice was thicker now. The barrel of the revolver lifted slightly and I could guess it was now pointed at my chest.

He stared at me and I tried to read his face, searching for the first sign of indecision. I thought I saw it and lowered my eyes toward the gun to see if it was turning away from me.

What I saw was his trigger finger tightening. I tensed —and the gun clicked. A misfire, and the life juices stirred in me and I stood up quickly and started for him.

And Vesuvius erupted in the room and something smashed my side, spinning me half around, and I heard another smashing roar and glass tinkled.

And before the lights went out I thought I heard another "click." And another and another . . . .

75

Chapter Nine

I came to on the studio couch. My side burned; I reached out a hand to touch it. My shirt was off and my fingers touched the bandages that covered a spot about over one of the middle ribs. My toes tingled, for some reason, and there was a steady ache behind my eyes.

". . . a .38 slug," some voice was saying. "We got it in pretty good shape. Must have caught the edges of two ribs before it passed on. Damn it, I'll bet it spun him like a top."

"Water?" I asked weakly.

"Hey, Sarge, he's coming to," the voice said, and then a cheerful young face came into my line of vision as he looked down at me. "Water, sir, coming right up."

He went away and a more familiar face came into view, my near-enemy, Sergeant Loepke. He looked down anxiously. "You all right?"

"I don't know, Sergeant. What are you doing here? This is Los Angeles."

"Donner, Sergeant Donner of the West Side Station thought I might be interested. I'm here with him. Who did it, Puma?"

"Robert Tampett, that son-of-a-bitch. I think he meant to kill me, Sergeant. The first time, his gun just clicked, so I went for him. Then there were two explosions and some more clicks. How many times was I hit?"

"Just once; jammed out a furrow between your ribs at the side. Took some splinters of bone along. Jesus, it could have been the end!"

I smiled. "You sound as though you cared, Sergeant. The last time I saw Captain Amos, he said Tampett couldn't be found. Was he found and released before he came here?"

Loepke shook his head.

"Somebody leaked to him," I said. "He came here, a gun in his hand, and accused me of putting the police on him. How did he know you boys were looking for him?"

76

Loepke's face stiffened. "You tell me."

The young interne came with the water, now, and helped me raise enough to drink some. The headache increased and I closed my eyes and pursed my lips.

I drank, and asked, "Aspirin? About four of 'em, maybe?"

"I'll bring you something better than that," he promised. He paused. "If you're not up to being questioned right now . . . ?"

"I'm up to it," I said. "I've been damaged more than this in bar fights."

He went away and Loepke's face was again in view. "Let's get back to your remark about a 'leak,' Puma," he said.

"Don't be so damned sensitive," I said. "Let's forget it. Maybe there wasn't a leak. We started this discussion real friendly, Sergeant."

"And then your big mouth got working and you implied we had a leak at Headquarters. I resent that kind of charge."

"Because you're honest," I explained. "But don't stand there and tell me you're so dumb you think all police officers are honest. I happen to know you're not that dumb. Can't we ever talk straight without a lot of phoney copy-book attitudes jamming up the lines? I admire you. I always have. I'll never like you, but I've always admired you."

"Come off it, Puma." He didn't believe me.

"Okay," I said resignedly. "So long, Sergeant. See you around."

He shook his head. "You have some questions to answer."

The interne came with the pills, and I said, "This talking is splitting my head. I guess I'd better rest, huh?"

He was only an interne, so he looked doubtfully at Sergeant Loepke.

Loepke said, "I'll keep my voice down, Joe. I'll be polite as long as you are. Don't forget, it's your assailant we'll be looking for, and any leads you can give us will help."

I took the pills and swallowed some more water and told the interne, "I guess a few minutes of quiet talk won't disturb me."

He looked relieved and went away.

"All right," I said. "Here's the way it was."

I gave it all to him, all of Tampett's monologue, and then went back before that and gave him the gist of my whole day.

"Foy," he said thoughtfully. "This Dr. Foy—he's outside of my jurisdiction but Sergeant Donner can work on that. How about Mrs. Richards? She's tied up some way with this Foy, if I remember."

"She's being treated by him," I answered, "and I want to ask you a favor about that, Sergeant. Until you get enough on him to book him, I don't want Mrs. Richards to know he's under suspicion."

He was silent, looking at me perplexedly.

"It's kind of complicated," I explained. "Somehow, quack though he is, he's helped Mrs. Richards psychologically. And she has a thing about him. I mean, he's some kind of symbol to her; she needs to believe in him. *Medically,* she needs to believe in him."

"You mean she's—punchy?" he asked.

"About Foy. As we all are, about this or that. Nothing personal, but I hope you don't think *you're* normal, Sergeant."

He opened his mouth and closed it.

"You're about as normal as I am," I said. "You have this antiquarian urge toward honesty and I have the temper of a three-year-old spoiled child. Neither of our afflictions are enough to put us in the loony bin, but they're not *normal.* Am I reaching you?"

"No," he said, "but you never do. I guess we live in different worlds, Puma."

"We do. But will you promise me not to alert Mrs. Richards about Foy?"

"I promise," he said.

Sergeant Donner came over to tell me he'd phone me in the morning to check on my ability to get down to the West Side Station. I told him there'd be no reason to phone; I could make it in the morning. They knew me at the West Side Station and trusted me.

And then, in a rare and touching moment of warmth, Sergeant Loepke reached over to pat my hand. "Don't worry, Puma," he said. "We'll get that damned Tampett!"

People—people and their contradictions. . . .

They left, taking my neighbor along, the one who had phoned them. The homeward-bound traffic outside hummed steadily, but it seemed unusually quiet in the room. My headache dimmed, but a strange uneasiness pricked at me.

I was startled by the jangle of the phone. I let it ring a few times, then answered it.

It was Fidelia. "Are we eating together? Or did you plan to make your report over the phone?"

"I'm resting," I said, "on the studio couch in my living room. I had a little accident."

"Accident? What kind?"

"I was shot about an hour ago. I'm all right. It was mostly shock. Nicked my ribs."

A silence, and then, "Joe, this isn't some horrible attempt at humor, is it?"

"Of course not," I said irritably. "Now, why—"

"You're so—so casual about it," she interrupted. "I mean—my God, Joe, *shot*?"

"Bob Tampett shot me," I said. "I'm sure he was drunk. And I probably wouldn't be talking to you now if his gun hadn't misfired a number of times."

"You stay right where you are," she said. "I'll bring over something special, exactly what you need."

Now, what could that be? I was sure she hadn't meant the first thing *my* mind had jumped to. Exactly what I needed? What I needed was more brains and less body.

What she brought was a thick soup. It was a lentil soup, made fresh every week at an expensive Brentwood delicatessen. I didn't have the heart to tell her I didn't like lentil soup.

"And cheese," she added, "and the best rye bread in town—all the strength-restoring foods." She leaned over to kiss my forehead, and then pulled a chair up next to the studio couch. "How are you feeling?"

"Okay. Shaky, and a little sore in the ribs, but that will go away." I studied her, wondering at her composure.

She read my glance and my mind. She exhaled, slumped and said, "I had to babble. I didn't want to break up.

79

And I had to keep telling myself you're—you're indestructible."

"See Foy today?" I asked her.

She shook her head. "I lied about the appointment. Why did you ask that?"

"When was the last time you had an appointment with him?"

She frowned. "Oh, it's been over a week. Joe, what's all this about?"

"I don't think you need him any more."

She stiffened. "What difference does it make? Joe, has something happened to him?"

I shook my head. "Not that I know of. I'm thinking of you, not of him. You've come through some bad moments with your chin up."

"You can thank Dr. Foy for that."

"For the bad moments, or the stiff chin?"

She was sitting rigidly now, staring at me doubtfully. "What are you trying to tell me? That Dr. Foy's a murderer?"

I shook my head slowly.

"Damn it!" she said tensely. "If you have something to tell me, do it openly. Don't play cat and mouse with my emotions. I can't take much of that."

"I'm sorry," I said quietly. "There's really nothing to tell. I guess it's that old animosity for Foy. I'm sorry. I'm glad you're here, Fidelia."

She sniffed. "That's more like it. I'll heat that soup. Are you sure you're all right, Joe?"

"There's nothing wrong that food won't cure."

She stood up and looked down at me for a moment with those candid, turquoise eyes. "Monster!" she said softly. "What a man." She went out to the kitchen.

I heard her moving around in there and wondered if I shouldn't have gone ahead and told her about Tampett and Foy. It seemed strange to me that she hadn't asked about Tampett; she hadn't asked me anything about Tampett's reasons for shooting me. That wasn't normal.

She came back into the living room and said, "It will only take a few minutes. Do you want to eat here?"

"No, we'll eat in the kitchen."

She sat down in the chair again. "What was Tampett

80

doing here? Did you have an appointment with him?"

I shook my head. "I was sitting right here, and the damned door opened and he walked in with a gun in his hand. He said I'd put the police onto him and—boom!"

"And as soon as I walked in, you started talking about Dr. Foy. Is there a connection, Joe?"

"Connection? Where?"

"Between Dr. Foy and Bob Tampett?"

I started to answer, and stopped. I looked at her thoughtfully.

"Tell me, if there is," she said.

"I have no proof that there is."

She rubbed her forehead and looked at the floor. "Another of your hunches?"

"Let's not talk about it tonight. I'm hungry and irritable."

"All right." She stroked my hair. "Puma, the indestructible. Puma, the avenging devil."

"Angel is the word," I corrected her. "It's avenging angel."

"Not Puma. Were you frightened when that gun was pointed at you?"

"I cringed. I whined."

"I'll bet." She leaned over and kissed me. "Are you weak? Are you helpless?"

"I'm hungry," I said. "Once I've eaten, I won't be weak. What did you do today?"

"I lounged around the pool, hoping somebody interesting would show up."

"And did someone?"

She made a face. "Tourists!" She nibbled my ear.

Lassitude moved through me, lassitude spiced with awareness. I asked, "Don't you have a home somewhere?"

"In Bel Air," she said, "but I never stay there. It's so isolated, up there in the hills." She caressed my jawline with her soft lips. "I rent it. I can use the income."

"Easy," I warned her. "I'm so hungry that I can't afford to get excited. I'd pass out."

She chuckled and stood up. "That soup should be hot enough now. You probably aren't a lentil soup fan, but this is going to be a new experience for you."

She was right. I had never had any lentil soup like *this,*

thick and rich, filling the stomach and replenishing the bloodstream, bringing back my manhood.

"Well?" she asked.

"Delicious," I agreed.

"A girl would never need to cook with soup like this for sale." She looked around. "And this place wouldn't be bad, with some new furniture."

I looked up, startled.

She laughed. "I was teasing." And then she looked at me gravely. "Would it be so horrible, married to me?"

"Only for you," I told her. "You could never get used to poverty, Fidelia."

"And you'd be too proud to live on my money?"

I pretended to give it some thought. "Well, maybe not. Maybe something could be worked out."

I saw the withdrawal in her face and this time I laughed. "Don't back off. It was your idea."

We were going after the cheese when my doorbell rang. It was Lou Serano.

He looked at me doubtfully. "I just got the word. Tampett came for you, eh?"

I nodded.

He looked at the roll and the cheese in my hand. "Eating?"

"No," I said, "I always walk around with food in my hand. I suppose you could use a cup of coffee?"

"If that's the best you have." He came in and followed me to the kitchen.

There, he looked at Fidelia and said, "Well, well, my favorite heiress! And eating paisan food."

Fidelia looked blankly at Lou and questioningly at me. "When did you two get to be buddies?"

Lou grinned. "When we learned we have a common enemy. Right, Puma?"

I nodded nervously.

"And who is the common enemy?" Fidelia asked quietly.

Lou looked at me, chagrin on his face. I said easily, "Robert Tampett."

"You're lying," she said. She looked at Lou, who was now seated at the table. "He is lying, isn't he?"

Glib Lou Serano, big-mouth Lou Serano, looked helplessly at me. He said nothing.

I met Fidelia's gaze. "I've explained to you, lady, that you must believe in me. I can't give you your money's worth unless you do." I sat down. "Let's have some coffee."

"Let's have some truth, first," she said evenly. "It's Dr. Foy you two are fighting, isn't it?"

Lou looked at the table top.

I said calmly, "I'm investigating everybody who could possibly be connected with the death of Brian Delsy. That's what you hired me to do, Fidelia. Do you want me to quit?"

She was breathing heavily now, her mouth slightly open. She licked her upper lip and stared between us.

"Even if you weren't paying me," I soothed her, "I'd be on your side. Damn it, either fire me or believe in me."

She continued to stare. Then suddenly she got up and went into the living room. I stood up and went to the doorway of the kitchen. I could see her from there. She opened her purse, took out a small bottle of pills, and headed for the bathroom.

"Fidelia," I called, "wait!"

She turned at the bathroom door. "Don't worry, I'm not going to do anything foolish. Ask your new friend Lou what's in the bottle."

From behind me, Lou said, "I know. It's all right, Joe."

I came back in to sit down. "What's she on?"

He shrugged. "Nothing dangerous. Seconal, allonal, veronal. One of the barbiturates. She's a high-strung girl."

"You know her pretty well, huh, Lou?"

He studied me. "Here we go again! Jealous? Hell, no, I don't know her the way your Latin mind is thinking. I know *about* her, because I'm trying to help her and I tried to learn *about* her. Calm down, hothead."

"You can say 'wop mind,' Lou. You're one, yourself."

"I'm sure as hell not an Arab." He poured himself some coffee. "I heard a weird one today—and from one of the weirdies."

"From one of the swishes?"

He nodded. "This punk swears that Brian Delsy learned something about Foy that burned him up and he was on his way over to tell Fidelia that on the night he was killed."

83

"Don't you think you or your informant should have given the police this information?"

He looked at me sourly. "Two of the many guys who don't go running to the law much could be Lou Serano and a queer. We haven't got your pipelines, Puma, and the law takes a dim view of us generally."

"Maybe the law would take a brighter view of you if you'd cooperate more."

He sighed and shook his head. "Oh, Lordy! Lectures, yet, from Muscles Puma. What the hell are *you* being so righteous about? You always work clean, maybe?"

"As clean as anyone in my profession."

He grinned. "Me, too. I'm the straightest hustler this side of the Rockies. Well, I just dropped in to see if you were okay." He finished his coffee and stood up. "I guess I'm never going to make your inner circle of friends, am I, Puma?"

"Thanks for what you've told me," I said. "And thanks for dropping around. I appreciate it."

I was walking to the door with him when Fidelia came out of the bathroom. She looked at both of us coolly. "Is the gossip session over, girls?"

Lou smiled at her and winked at me. "Be good, kids." He went out, closing the door behind him.

Fidelia said, "I thought you couldn't stand hoodlums."

"He's no friend of mine, honey. I didn't invite him here. But I'll use any ally I can find when I'm looking for a killer."

She went into the kitchen and sat down again. She poured herself some fresh coffee.

I sat across from her. "How many pills did you take?"

"Two. Two aspirin."

"Honestly, Fidelia?"

She didn't answer. She asked, "What did Lou tell you? What did he tell you that I should know?"

"He told me he heard that Delsy was on his way to see you when he was killed. That's the kind of information I'm trying to keep from you. I'm supposed to be your *shield*, remember?"

She expelled her breath. "Okay, okay, okay. I'm sorry."

A silence. I drank coffee, she drank coffee. From the apartment next door came the sound of a news report on

84

TV. Outside, traffic went buzzing by. But in my little rat's-nest, silence.

She looked up and her gaze held mine gravely. She said, "We were so cozy here and then that—then *he* had to come along."

"The night is young," I consoled her. "Have some more cheese."

"Stomach," she said. "You're all stomach and mouth and biceps. Damn your insensitive soul."

I stood up, began to pick up the dishes. As I reached for one at her end of the table, the bandage pulled, and I winced.

"Joe!" she said quickly. "Don't do that. I'll pick up the dishes. You go and relax. Joe—please?"

I smiled my forgiving, martyr's smile and went into the living room and back to the studio couch. I thought back on the visit of Lou Serano and realized I should have pressed him for more details about Brian Delsy's motives in coming to see Fidelia. I would have to talk further with Lou. Or his informant.

An easy assumption could be that Delsy, also a patient of Foy's, had learned something detrimental to the good doctor's reputation. But Fidelia had been hearing that sort of thing from professional sources; she was well aware of what other people thought of Foy.

It was dark outside now and the headlights from Wilshire Boulevard made moving patterns on the wall I was facing. Big, bustling, buzzing, humming, continually moving town. Where were they all going? Some place they hadn't been? Some place they'd never find?

Fidelia came in from the kitchen and sat in the chair next to the couch. She stared quietly out the window at the headlights.

Finally, she said, "Are you brooding?"

I shook my head. "Thinking." I smiled at her. "About you, mostly."

"I'm a brat," she said. "But you're not the most rational man in the world."

"I know. I was explaining that to Sergeant Loepke late this afternoon. Come over here and stroke my hair again."

"You know where that will lead," she warned me. "And we don't know if you're well enough."

85

"If I start to get weak, I'll warn you," I promised. "I'm lonely. Aren't you?"

"I took some seconal," she said. "I'd fall asleep, and humilate you. Joe, is sex your answer to *everything*?"

"Lacking money, yes. Where else, today, do you find a really honest communication?"

"P. I. Puma," she mocked me, "the slant-head's philosopher."

I moved over closer to the wall and stretched out. I watched the lights play over her face and tried to imagine her youth, tried to guess what kind of childhood the rich had, what kind of fun.

The only light in the room was the dimly reflected light from the kitchen and the passing lights from the cars. All around us were other small and occupied apartments, but it was momentarily peaceful here, possibly because we were the only humans in sight who weren't moving.

"I guess I'm not going to fall asleep," Fidelia said finally. She came over to stretch out next to me. "Be gentle."

Chapter Ten

Rich foods and indolence; her body should be soft and white, sagging and passive. But her body was golden and firm, resistant and demanding.

Slow now, easy and gentle. . . . Above us, on the wall, the reflections of all those seeking headlights came and went, came and went. . . .

And then the great shudder and the great sigh and she murmured, almost too quietly to hear, "I don't need him, I don't need him, I don't need him, any more."

I didn't ask her whom she didn't need. I hoped it was Foy.

She fell asleep and I covered her with a blanket and slept in my own bed, slept straight through until morning. I didn't even open my eyes until almost nine o'clock.

There was no overcast in the morning. The sun was out and the smog light. I went into the living room, but the studio couch was unoccupied. My lady had left in the night. On the rumpled pillow, one auburn hair glistened in the morning sunlight.

I was getting out my king-sized frying pan when the doorbell rang. I went to the door and asked, "Who's there?"

"Loepke," he said, and I opened it to let him in.

"I'm just about to fry some eggs," I told him. "Could you go for a couple?"

He shook his head. "I could use a cup of coffee, though."

I made him a cup of instant coffee. He sat at the end of the table in the kitchen and said, "We gave Los Angeles that slug that killed Delsy and they compared it with the one that nicked you." He paused. "Same gun."

I turned from the stove where I was frying my eggs. "That should nail Tampett—if we can find him."

"It should," he shrugged, "but Tampett's covered for the time Delsy died."

"How could he be? He told me he left the bar and came home. He lives alone. How could he be covered?"

"He came back to his apartment house, but not home. There was a party going on two apartments down the hall and he spent the next three hours there."

"He didn't tell me that. He said he came home."

"That's what he told us, at first, too. I suppose he didn't want to tell us about the party because his neighbors would know what he was when we questioned them. Well, since he disappeared, we went back and questioned the neighbors anyway." He held out his hands, palms up. "And we come up with this. Which leaves us where?"

"With lying neighbors," I answered.

He shook his head. "Two of the people at the party were real solid citizens. Now, with you, Tampett figured to kill you, I'm sure, so there still wouldn't be any lead to the gun. And most of the time, the slugs are too smashed up to compare, anyway."

I sat down with my eggs and toast.

Sergeant Loepke said, "Ye gods! how many eggs did you fry?"

"Six," I said. "I've been sick, Sergeant. I was shot. I have to regain my strength if I'm going out to hunt Tampett."

For the first time, he half smiled. "What a man. Could I make myself another cup of this coffee?"

"Be my guest," I said. "The water's still hot."

As he was mixing the coffee, he said musingly, "I suppose a man needs to know you a long time in order to like you."

"You never would," I told him. "You're an honest man, Sergeant."

He came back with the cup of coffee and sat down. "And you're not?"

"I am, but at a different level. Nothing personal, but it's a higher level. I may use shoddy means to achieve a worthwhile end."

"That's not right, and you know it. That's not honest."

"Of course it isn't, not in the old-fashioned sense. Basically, it's wrong. But it's the only possible way to survive in this world of today and still sleep nights."

He shook his head stubbornly.

"It's the way," I told him, "this world has been kept in one piece since 1932. It's the new mid-century honesty, Sergeant, and you'll starve if you don't go along with it."

"I'm not starving," he said.

"For a man of your abilities, you are. You should have been a lieutenant six years ago, and you know it."

He was silent. He studied me.

I smiled at him.

"I always figured you for a dumb, loud, tough wop, and nothing more," he said finally.

"I am," I said simply. "Dumb, loud, tough—and hungry."

He sipped his coffee and closed his eyes wearily.

I asked, "How late did you work last night?"

He shrugged. "What difference does it make? I *like* to work. What else is there?"

"A whole big, fat world full of wine, women and song."

"Not for me," he said. "Are you going after this Tampett?"

I smiled. "With both hands, Sergeant. As soon as I finish these eggs."

"You remember," he warned me, "you're not the law. You remember that, Puma."

"I am the law, Sergeant. Every citizen is the law. The

88

others don't work at it like we do, but we're the only law there is."

He stood up. "Who can talk sense to you? Thanks for the coffee. You—mug! At least, be careful. You can promise me that much, can't you?"

I winked at him. "Sergeant, believe it or not, my first instinct is self-preservation. I'll be very careful."

"Don't open any doors, from either side, without a gun in your hand."

I nodded. "You should have told me that yesterday morning. Carry on, Sergeant. You're a good man and we need you."

"You might even be one, yourself," he admitted. "Who can tell, today?" He went out, closing the door quietly behind him.

A servant of the people, Sergeant Daniel Loepke. Despised, underpaid, demeaned and resented, a servant of the people, the miserable, stinking people.

While the hoodlums ran the world. Why did I hate the hoodlums so much? Because so many of them were Italian, and I hated myself? How could I hate myself, a wonderful guy like me?

I had just finished shaving when the phone rang. It was Mrs. Foy.

"I read in the paper this morning about Bob Tampett," she said. "Who's next? Am I next?"

"Why should you be? Has he bothered you?"

"No. But he came for you because of Arnie, didn't he? Because you were a threat to Arnie? And who gave you the dope on Arnie?"

"You were a big help to me, Mrs. Foy," I said, "but what you told me about the Doctor was something any investigator could have learned without going to you. It simply would have taken longer. A number of people know Dr. Foy is a fake. The ones he worries about are the people who know it and intend to do something about it."

"You think I'm safe, then?"

"I couldn't guarantee you that. If you can afford it, you might get out of the house for a couple of days."

"I can afford it. I've got a few friends left. Puma, will they catch him? Tampett, I mean."

89

"I'm sure they will. I'm looking for him, too."

"Fine," she said. "Fine." A pause. "Some day, when this is all over, drop around, huh?"

"I'm looking forward to it," I said. "Chin up, now."

"Sure," she said. "Good luck, Puma."

A number of people had undoubtedly lied to me; I should have recorded my conversations in a notebook for cross-verification. Some day, I would have to get organized and be an efficient investigator.

One statement that seemed like a lie had been voiced by Willis Morley, and there was only one place to check that—the law offices of Gallegher, Hartford and Leedom in Beverly Hills.

They were dignified and impressive offices and so was the girl in the waiting room—her manner dignified, her body impressive. I wondered which of the partners had chosen *her*.

"Mr. Puma?" she said, and frowned. "Did you have an appointment with Mr. Gallegher?"

"No. I'm here in the interest of Mrs. Fidelia Sherwood Richards. Why don't you tell him that?"

She didn't use the phone on her desk; she excused herself and disappeared down a corridor.

While she was gone, a young man came in, looked at me in doubtful recognition and then came over to where I was standing. It was the attorney who had represented Fidelia in Chief Nystrom's office.

"Mr. Puma," he said genially. "Could I be of service?"

"I'm waiting to see Mr. Gallegher," I told him. "Nothing personal, but he probably knows more about what I want to know."

"I'm sure he does," the young man agreed. "How is Mrs. Richards reacting to all this recent publicity?"

"Like a Marine sergeant," I said. "I think she needs that Foy like I need fifty more pounds."

He laughed. "One thing you must remember about Mrs. Richards, she's an extremely loyal girl. It's her dominant trait."

From the mouths of babes . . . I looked at him in awe. "By golly," I said, "I'll bet you would have graduated *cum laude* from Sunset College of Clinical Psychology."

90

His smile put me back into my peasant world. "I did —from Harvard." He nodded. "Good morning, Mr. Puma."

I stood there, conscious of my thick ankles, until the girl came back to tell me Mr. Gallegher would see me now.

T. Winfield Gallegher looked to me like an Irishman who was 'passing'. At a certain level, these sturdy sons of common stock occasionally adopted the mannerisms and attitudes of their natural enemy. The "T" must stand for Terrence, I thought. Thomas could be mistaken for an English name.

His accent was faintly British, his tailoring Savile Row, his manner gentle. He was tall and bony and probably hoping for warts.

"Mr. Puma," he said, smiling. "I'm an admirer of yours, sir. I have followed your exploits in the press with great interest." He indicated a chair, after shaking my hand.

"Thank you, Mr. Gallegher," I said in my Fresno best. "The man who concerns me today is Willis Morley."

A faint flicker of distaste showed briefly on the aristocratic face across the desk. "Oh, yes."

"I have reason to think he lied to me," I went on. "He told me, in his office, that you had suggested he try to wean Mrs. Richards away from the influence of Dr. Arnold Foy."

T. Winfield Gallegher straightened in his chair and his Irish blue eyes flashed fire. "That is far from the truth. That is a damned lie!"

"I thought it might be. Did he initially suggest it to you?"

"He mentioned it to me, yes. I voiced neither approval nor disapproval."

"Why would he lie?" I asked.

His face became guarded. "I have no idea. I would think it unwise to venture an opinion."

"Mr. Gallegher," I said patiently. "We're alone here. Nobody is taking dictation and we can speak in complete confidence without any fear of reprisal from anyone. Our mutual interest is the well-being of Mrs. Fidelia Sherwood Richards. It is no time for either courtroom dignity or the impediment of involved ethics."

91

He stared at me thoughtfully for a moment.

"A man is dead," I went on, "and Mrs. Richards is in possible peril. Both of us represent her in our separate and disparate ways. We're allies, Mr. Gallegher—you have to believe that."

He opened his mouth and closed it. He opened it again and said, "I do believe that, Mr. Puma. I may have reason to regret your—your *modus operandi,* but never have I doubted your essential integrity."

"Thank you," I said solemnly, and waited.

He licked his lips. "Mr. Morley is a shrewd and persuasive man. His unusually benign façade is no doubt very effective in lulling his—his clients into a false sense of confidence. Mrs. Richards trusts him implicity."

"Does he resemble her father?"

T. Winfield Gallegher stiffened again. "Not in *any* way. Mr. Sherwood was an uncommonly distinguished gentleman. Well, to get on, *and this is in strictest confidence,* I have a feeling Mr. Morley assumes he will be in charge of the Sherwood estate when Mrs. Richards comes into it."

"Brother!" I said. "And wouldn't he milk it?"

T. Winfield Gallegher looked bleakly into space and did not comment.

"What possible reason," I mused aloud, "would Willis Morley have for trying to convince me this suggestion about Foy came from you?"

"I have no idea," he said, "but I'm sure you have."

"I do," I admitted and stood up. "Mr. Gallegher, thank you."

He rose and extended his hand across the desk. "Mr. Puma, good luck. Carry on, sir, in the finest Puma tradition."

I went out with banners flying, chin up, ego restored. I paused at the desk of the girl with the body, and asked lightly, "Do you like to dance?"

"I love it," she said. "Every Tuesday and Saturday night my husband and I go square dancing."

Square dancing! Oh, boy. What a monstrous waste.

I was only a few blocks from the office and I called Fidelia from there.

When she answered, I asked lightly, "What time did you leave?"

"This morning. You were snoring."

"Easy, lady; this goes through the hotel switchboard."

"I forgot." A pause. "I miss you. Are you working?"

"I am. I've just come from your lawyer's office. While I was there, I remembered something you told me that didn't check with what somebody else told me."

"Oh?"

"You told me you learned about Willis Morley through an ad in the *Times*. He told me he was recommended to you by a mutual friend."

A long silence.

"Are you still there?" I asked.

"Yes, yes." Another silence. "He told the truth. I was introduced to him through a mutual friend."

"Why did you lie?"

I could hear her intake of breath. "Because this—this mutual friend asked me not to mention it. He said it might be misunderstood. At that time, his word was law to me."

"At that time? You're talking about Dr. Foy? He was the mutual friend, wasn't he?"

"He was." A pause. A long one, but I didn't fill it. Finally, she said, "I think I'm cured of him, Joe. I'm not sure, though, but I—"

"You're a very loyal girl, Fidelia. You musn't think of that as any kind of flaw."

"It's more than loyalty, though. It's a dependence, an absurd, pathological dependence."

"It *was*." I hesitated, and then asked, "Tell me, did you ever think of him romantically? I mean, did you ever contemplate marrying him."

"Not definitely. I mean, I have a feeling it eventually could have led to that. You don't think— I mean, could he have been planning to make me *that* dependent on him?"

My impulse was to say "yes," but it might be too early. I said, "Who knows? I don't."

A silence again. And then, "I think I'll go over to the pool. Do you *have* to work?"

"I do. You go get the sun. Maybe I can make it for lunch."

"Try to," she said. "I won't expect you, but try to."

I promised her I would and hung up. Who was I, the

93

new Dr. Foy? I headed for Venice and the humble abode of Snip Caster.

Snip lived in a ramshackle rooming house run by a retired prostitute on a back lot off one of Venice's discarded canals. He was addicted to muscatel and at the bottom of the social ladder. But in his palmier days little Snip had enjoyed some big-league mobster associations. They had forgotten him now, luckily for Snip, but he still kept his ears open.

His landlady, a haggard old crow, was hanging some clothes in the side yard as I parked in the packed-earth parking area behind the front of the house.

She looked at me with suspicion. She was sweet on Snip and resented any outsiders who might make him solvent enough to leave the neighborhood.

"Snip in his room?" I asked her.

"Look for yourself," she told me. "This ain't no hotel."

"Why, Aggie," I said, "I'm not here to take him away. I'm a friend of his."

She sniffed and gave her attention to the clothes she was stringing on the line.

"Snip should buy you a dryer," I said.

"With what?" she asked. "Empty muscatel bottles?"

Poor Snip. As recently as fifteen years ago, he had been squiring starlets around. And now he had Aggie.

I went up the worn steps to the small room in the rear and found him paging through a girlie magazine.

His thin face lighted up and he asked, "You bring a bottle? Buddie, buddie, buddie! You must have brought a bottle."

I handed him a dollar. "I forgot. Get your own. Snip, you know where Eddie's is, don't you? You know the place?"

He nodded. "I know the place. And Eddie. So?" He held up a hand. "Hey, wait! You're working on that Delsy kill."

"I am."

"For money, big money, huh? For that Sherwood dame, I bet."

"It's possible."

He shook his head. "And you slip me a lousy buck. Big shot Puma!"

94

"The buck was for old times, Snip. How do I know if you can do me any good?"

"Ask me and find out," he said.

"I'm looking for a man named Robert Tampett," I said. "Know him?"

"Yup."

"Know where he is now?"

He shook his head.

"All right, give me the buck back. Drink water this week."

He smiled, his thin face sly. "The buck was for old times. Maybe I could find out where this Tampett is. What's it worth?"

"A fin, a sawbuck, maybe."

"And you get?"

"I'm working for my client at a reduced rate. This Tampett is more of a personal search. He shot me, Snip. He tried to kill me."

His eyes widened. "That foolish man. He should have made sure, or got out of the country, huh?"

I said nothing, looking modestly Herculean.

"I'll nose around," he said. "A sawbuck—that's tops?"

"Maybe more, if I can put it on the expense account. Be careful, though, Snip. You get a couple belts in you and you run off at the mouth too much."

"Job like this, I drink later," he assured me. "I'll get in touch." He looked around and lowered his voice. "And don't tell Aggie you gave me the buck."

I promised him I wouldn't.

The pattern was in my mind, now, the pattern that revolved around Fidelia Sherwood Richards. And it made Tampett a key figure, the tool of the Machiavellian Foy, a man with no local record who had risked killing me. The stakes must be high to drive Tampett to murder.

As I went to my car, Aggie called, "How much did you give him?"

"Nothing yet," I answered. "He has to earn it, first."

She sniffed suspiciously. "That'll be the day."

I smiled at her and got into my car and headed downtown, toward the forty-per-cent Santa Claus.

Chapter Eleven

All I had was the pattern. Perhaps a case could be tailored from it and perhaps not. People lie for a number of reasons, as I have said before. Out of ego and spite, malice and petulance, people lie. But if the truth can save their necks, they finally resort to it.

Chubby Willis Morley was no fool and perhaps he could be pressed to give me more truth than he had so far if I pointed out that the percentage might be in his favor.

Intangibles I had, but intangibles are meaningless in court. There was no point in finding a killer unless he could be convicted.

The smog grew stronger and the traffic heavier. There had been very little smog in Beverly Hills but the sky was yellow ahead. I should have phoned; it was a miserable trip to take for nothing.

But it wasn't all for nothing: Willis Morley was in his office, talking earnestly with an elderly and apparently nervous woman. The door to his waiting room was open; he came over to nod to me and then close it.

I sat with a copy of *Life,* framing my approach in my mind, checking back for inconsistencies and contradictions, a lever to use on this pompous pirate.

The only opening I had was his claim that Fidelia's lawyers had approached him on Foy. That wasn't much, and easily open to argument. Well, I'd tell him what I had and await a reaction.

Lacking the authority of the municipal man, reaction was my only weapon. I could nose around and nose around until somebody got nervous and made a foolish move. Tampett had already made one, but it had hurt me more than it had him.

I had left *Life* and was working on *Newsweek* when Willis brought the elderly woman through and to the door to the corridor. "Don't you worry, now," he told her. "Everything's going to be just fine."

96

His smile faded as he closed the door behind her and turned to face me. "Well, Mr. Puma?"

"I thought we could talk," I said. "I have an interesting theory for your slide rule."

He frowned. "I have another appointment in ten minutes. How much time do you need?"

"Ten minutes might do it—if you don't interrupt?"

His frown deepened. "You're not making much sense, Mr. Puma."

I stood up. "Let's go into your office and I'll try to."

He stood there quietly in indecision, his blue eyes probing my face. Then he nodded toward the door to his office. He followed me in and closed the door behind him.

He went over to sit behind his desk and I sat in the chair recently occupied by the elderly woman.

"All right, Mr. Puma," he said solemnly, "let's hear this theory of yours."

"It concerns a rich and emotionally erratic girl," I began, "who went to a quack psychologist for treatment. She developed an unhealthy attachment for this man. And the quack, being what he was, put his cunning mind to work. There should be, he figured, some way to get into the girl's money a lot faster than he could through his fees for treatment."

In his chair, Willis Morley stirred and his blue eyes blinked nervously. He said nothing.

"This quack," I went on, "had a friend who knew his way around money, a loan shark with a most benevolent exterior, and the quack sent his patient to this knowing man, generously aware that the girl had enough money for two needy pirates and it would be smarter to have her estate robbed by an expert."

Willis Morley bristled. "Just one second, Mr. Puma!"

"It's only a theory," I said soothingly. "There's no need to be alarmed unless it's true."

He subsided in his chair, glaring at me.

"However," I continued, "under treatment, the girl became more and more dependent on the quack. And it occurred to him that if he married the girl, and it certainly seemed possible, he would be in a position to enjoy her money without the need of sharing with outsiders. Avarice entered the picture."

97

Willis Morley said stiffly, "My books are open to any authorized accounting at any time."

"You're interrupting," I chided him. "So the first thing the quack does is convince the girl she shouldn't reveal that he had sent her to the loan expert. And then he has her move to another address, to confuse the loan man further. The loan man begins to see the picture, so he hires a private investigator to look up the girl and find out what's cooking. In comes Puma." I paused. "Blind."

"Borrowers," said Willis stiffly, "are required to inform their creditors of any change of address."

"A solid point," I agreed. "So, back at the ranch, an unfortunate patient of the quack's named Brian Delsy learns of this alliance between the psychologist and the loan broker and realizes what is happening to a girl whom, for some perverse reason, he admires."

Willis fidgeted and looked at his watch.

"At a bar in Venice," I breezed on, "this troubled man tries to get the girl to his booth so he can inform her of the alliance, but he is not successful. The girl leaves and the patient is thrown out of the joint by the bartender. He is a little drunk by this time and still determined to reveal all to the girl. However, it takes him a while to learn her new address."

Willis looked at his watch again.

"If it's time for that appointment," I said, "I can leave."

"Go on," he said. "I'm listening."

"But," I said ominously, "the man named Delsy is not careful. He doesn't realize the stakes involved and possibly doesn't know that a friend of his, a hustler named Robert Tampett, is actually in the employ of the quack. And this Tampett knows that if the girl learns about the alliance, all the girl's lovely money will stay at home, where he figures it doesn't belong."

"So Robert Tampett killed Delsy, then?" Willis Morley asked.

"It seems logical, doesn't it?"

He didn't answer, staring into space.

"But Tampett's covered, accordng to the police," I said. "So who's our next choice, Mr. Morley?"

He stared at me and said nothing.

"Note shaving and usury aren't likely to get you into

trouble," I said gently. "They're the order of the day. But *murder,* Mr. Morley?"

His round face was like rock. "Don't be absurd. Certaintly, you don't think me capable of murder."

"Why did you lie to me?" I asked him.

"Lie? When did I lie to you?"

"When you told me Mrs. Richards' attorneys suggested to you that you influence her away from Foy. I talked with Mr. Gallegher this morning and he assured me that was not the way it happened. You suggested it to Mr. Gallegher."

"I did nothing of the kind. Certainly, you don't expect a man of Mr. Gallegher's station to admit he was interfering in the medical treatment of a client?"

I said nothing.

Morley took a deep breath. "You have a theory, involved and fictional. That's all you have and it would be laughed out of any court in the state. Why did you bring it here?"

"Because I think it's possible you are not the murderer. And if you aren't, it might be in your best interest to help me find out who is."

He looked at his watch for the third time. "I've given you all the time I can, Mr. Puma. Good day to you."

I stood up. "You're underestimating me, Mr. Morley. I'm not something you can figure with that slide rule. I'm human, and there's vengeance in me."

"You're being melodramatic," he said, "and adolescent. *Good day,* sir." He stood up.

He wasn't frightened. He glared at me, a bristling, overweight rooster, ferocious and unfrightened. So far as I could tell.

"Don't strike me," I murmured. "I'll go quietly."

"And don't come back," he said.

Another account lost. I went out into the smog and down the dirty street to my car. Where was I? Nowhere.

I was a simple Fresno peasant, unequipped to cope with the sharp and cunning tigers I met in my trade. All I had were my muscles and my mouth and my hazy peasant intuition. They weren't enough.

Of course, I had this elusive Latin charm that occasionally served as a weapon. But never with men, damn it!

99

Except with men like Brian Delsy, possibly, but Brian was dead.

"Dead, dead, dead," I repeated to myself, and passers-by on the sidewalk looked at me curiously, compassionately or scornfully, depending on their moods and personalities.

The Plymouth seemed to sneer at me as she coughed into life. Where was I? On Figueroa Street, heading for Olympic. I could have used the freeway, but I never do. That was where the real tigers roamed, the wholesale killers.

Tampett. I had to find Tampett. I had to find him and get his throat between my hands and choke some truth out of him. How else was I equipped to operate, a peasant like me?

My sore side itched and my sinuses ached and I reflected that I was working on this miserable case at half-pay. What a jerk was Joe Puma!

The Plymouth seemed to steer itself to Santa Monica and the Avalon Beach. Fidelia was having lunch on the deck above the pool.

She wore a terry-cloth robe over her Bikini and she wore a smile for her glowering knight.

"Well?" she asked.

"Nobody, nothing, nowhere," I said. I sat in the chair across the table from her. "I've got to find Tampett."

"Of course you do," she agreed. "So you can bruise and batter him and hear him cry out for mercy."

"Right!" I said.

"My lion," she said, "Joe Puma."

"Your dope, Joe Puma. I'm stupid and meaningless."

"Of the three, only arrogant," she said. "Joe, you need a drink."

I nodded and leaned back.

"Gin and tonic," she told the waiter, "in a tall, tall glass. And bring a luncheon menu for my guest."

The waiter went away and Fidelia smiled at me. "My fort, my shield, my good right arm and tender lover, Joe Puma."

Your new Doctor Foy, I thought, but didn't say. Was that why Tampett tried to kill me? I was less of an in-

100

vestigative threat than a substitute perhaps, but a substitute could be more damaging to their cause.

"What are you thinking?" she asked me.

"Everything and nothing. Did you have any visitors today?"

"Lou Serano phoned. He said he'd phone again. He wants to talk with you." She grimaced. "I like him less every minute."

The waiter came back with my drink and a menu. I ordered the beef Stroganoff.

At the far end of the pool, poised on the diving board, a girl with an exquisite figure drew my attention. Fidelia turned to examine the target of my glance and then looked sharply back at me. The blue-green eyes glinted, but she said nothing.

Her fort, her shield, her tender lover—and her proud possession? I smiled at her; her answering smile was forced.

"Muscles and mouth, I called you," she reminded me. "I forgot you also have an eye."

"I try not to miss anything," I said agreeably. The cool drink went down, easing my tensions.

"It would be *hell*, married to you," she said, after a few seconds. "You were never married, were you?"

"Not even once," I admitted.

"You have all the instincts of a tomcat," she continued.

Her fort, her shield and her tender lover—and her pin cushion?

I said, "You're working yourself up into a peeve. Would you want to tell me why?"

"Did you have to say you weren't married even *once*. Was that a nice thing to say to me?"

"No. But it had no meaning. I just said it."

"Did you have to look at that girl on the diving board?"

"Yes. For some reason I can't stop smoking or looking at girls on diving boards. Fidelia, it's pleasant here and this drink has helped me and the food will help even more. Do we have to quibble?"

A pause, while she looked at me gravely. Then she smiled and said, "Not if you sit in this chair and I sit in yours."

101

So we changed chairs and now she was facing the board and the most pleasant thing in my line of vision was she. The waiter brought my food and her iced coffee.

We were silent for minutes, which I didn't mind, because I was hungry and it was first-class beef Stroganoff. The electricity of emotional turbulence was in the air, though, and I had a sense of uneasiness.

She said, "You slurp when you eat. Can't you stop that?"

I smiled at her. "I'll try. I come from a family of slurpers. Am I no longer your fort, your shield, your tender lover and good right arm?"

She looked down at the table. She was trembling slightly. Her voice was low. "I don't know what gets into me. I think I'd better phone Dr. Foy."

"You've gone through a bad time," I told her, "and handled it all without him. You're loyal and beautiful and courageous and even fairly intelligent, for a woman. Don't expect to be perfect; even Dr. Freud never expected people to be that. What do you need that you haven't got?"

"Stability," she said. "Emotional stability."

"Jesus!" I said.

"And what's wrong with that?"

I shook my head. "You've just told me you want to be a cow. Honey, you haven't the build for it."

"You're a bull," she said, "and you seem happy."

"I'm not a bull. I never paw around. I'm a tomcat and a hedonist, a voyeur and an idiot, but I'm not a bull. Is that iced coffee any good?"

"It's excellent," she said, "Mr. Stomach!"

I signalled the waiter and ordered some iced coffee.

She leaned back and closed her eyes. I turned around to see if the diving board was occupied. It wasn't. The waiter brought my iced coffee and Fidelia's eyes were still closed.

"Do you want me to quit looking for Tampett?" I asked her.

Her eyes opened and she stared at me curiously. "Why should I? What a strange question!"

"I was simply trying to get the dialogue back to the subject that should be concerning us."

She closed her eyes again. "The subject bores me.

102

Sending a man to the gas chamber won't bring Brian back. I may take you off the case." She opened her eyes. "And then you'd have to scratch up another client."

"Don't patronize me, Fidelia Sherwood Richards. Not at half-pay and on the cuff."

She continued to stare at me. I stared back. She smiled and I didn't.

"Do I apologize now?" she asked quietly.

"I'm just an employee, Mrs. Richards. Suit yourself."

"Damn you!" she said fiercely. "You're a self-sufficient son-of-a-bitch, aren't you?"

I shook my head. "Self-reliant, maybe. Like you're getting, more every day. Let's be nice. It's too hot to fight."

"All right," she said tiredly. "All right, all right. Could we go and hear Pete play tonight?"

"At Eddie's? Is he still there?"

She nodded.

"I'll buy the steaks, tonight," I soothed her. "I'll be your tender lover."

"I'm sorry," she said. "I want to—to own people. Joe, you find that Bob Tampett and shake the truth out of him. And don't despise me."

"Never," I promised. "Even at half-pay, I love you, Fidelia Sherwood Richards."

She blew me a kiss and I kept my eyes carefully away from the diving board as I smiled at her and went back to my working world. Lou Serano had left no number to call and I couldn't hang around indefinitely. From a phone in the lobby of the Avalon Beach, I called my answering service.

Snip had been busy; he had left an address and a message. The address was 218 Alta Canal and the message was *Don't forget the sawbuck. I'm thirsty.*

I had given him a dollar and the stuff he drank was only eighty-nine cents a half-gallon. How could he be thirsty?

The address was east of Main Street in Venice, not too far from the lodging house where Snip lived, though on a different canal. It was a tiny and ancient pseudo-Spanish structure, the stucco cracked and peeling, half the tiles missing from the roof.

On the gray grass side yard, an ebony Cadillac convertible was parked. It looked like Lou Serano's car to me.

I took out my gun and went carefully along the walk that led to the front door, which faced on the canal. I could hear footsteps in the house as I went along that side of it, and as I got to the front of the house, Lou Serano came out onto the porch.

I stopped and he stopped. He was pale and his glance went nervously to the gun in my hand and then up to meet my gaze.

"I'm looking for Tampett," I said. "Is he in there?"

He nodded.

"Is this your house, Lou?"

He shook his head.

"What's the matter?" I asked him irritably. "Can't you talk?"

He nodded toward the door, still open behind him. "Take a look."

I went up the steps and through the open doorway into a small living room, furnished in wicker and rattan. Robert Tampett was lying on his side on the raffia rug in there.

There was a hole above his left ear. There wasn't an awful lot of blood; he had died quickly.

Chapter Twelve

I came out to the porch again. Lou stood there, staring at the dry, trash-littered canal.

"Who did it, Lou?" I asked.

He shrugged, still staring at the canal.

"How did you know he was here? Did you come here, looking for him?"

He nodded.

"How long ago?"

He turned to face me. "A couple minutes, seconds ago. I don't know. What the hell, you don't think I—?"

"Turn around," I said, "and put your hands up on that post."

He stared at me. "Are you crazy?"

"Hurry," I said.

He turned around and put his hands high on one of the pillars that supported the roof of the porch. I frisked him and found nothing. I asked, "Is there a phone here? Does it work?"

He shrugged.

"Let's go in and see," I said. "You first."

There was a phone in the house, but it was dead. The place had that vacancy smell and the dust was heavy on all the window sills.

I debated it in my mind and finally told Lou, "You get to the nearest phone and call the police. I'll stay here. And don't take off, or you'll be in serious trouble."

He nodded. "Don't worry; I'll call 'em."

The room in the Venice Station smelled of cigar smoke, though Sergeant Macrae wasn't smoking. He was a sour, thin-faced Scotsman, an excellent officer, hard-working, cynical and efficient.

"You and murder," he said. "Why do they always go together?"

"Most of my cases have nothing to do with murder, Sergeant. You only see me on the Venice jobs and murder seems to be routine down here lately."

He looked at me sharply, "What do you mean, *lately?* Was that a crack?"

"You know it wasn't," I said softly. "It's a bad time."

He picked up my report from the desk in front of him. "I see you didn't check Serano's car for a gun. Now, why not?"

"I guess," I said humbly, "because I'm a lousy investigator. But, hell, would he be hanging around the house if he'd already been out to his car?"

"So," he said, "next question—where's Serano now?"

I said nothing, looking at the top of his desk.

"Didn't you tell him to wait for us?" he asked.

"I told him to call you. I assumed he'd wait. Taking off like he did would be a dumb move. Didn't he identify himself when he phoned?"

"Hell, yes. He identified himself as Joe Puma. Well, we'll get him. And he won't run, next time."

"I warned him about taking off," I said. "He must have

105

thought I meant he shouldn't take off without phoning. You see, Sergeant, he's a hustler and I'm sure that right now he's seeking first-class legal advice. His lawyer will bring him in."

"What was he doing there?"

"I don't know. I can only guess. The guess is in the report, in that background sheet I added."

An officer came in and handed Macrae my gun and also a small sheet of paper, probably a ballistics report.

Macrae looked at the report and handed me back my gun.

"Clear?" I asked him.

He sniffed. "Not by a damned sight. Puma, I wish to hell you'd stay in the other end of town."

"Sergeant," I reminded him softly, "you have a short memory. Didn't I get you a whole front page of publicity last time we worked together? Didn't I wrestle that freak Devine for your Pension Fund? You owe me more courtesy than I'm getting, Sergeant Macrae."

The officer grinned. Sergeant Macrae glowered and told the officer. "Okay, you can go."

The officer was still grinning as he went out.

Macrae said, "Mouthy as ever, aren't you? I'm surprised your face isn't marked up more."

"I've got a nasty slice between my ribs that Robert Tampett put there."

"I know," he said. "So then you're found in the same house with him and he's dead. And *everybody* knows about your temper. Now, isn't it reasonable that you should be in jail this second? Think like a police officer for one second and then answer."

"Serano will clear me. Wait until he shows."

"Serano, hell! How do we know you didn't kill Tampett some time ago and then come back?"

"Do you know when Tampett died?"

He shook his head. "Not yet. But if and when we do, you'd better be ready with a story, Puma."

"Easy, now," I said. "You're sounding like a cop out of a B picture, Sergeant. You know me and you know my reputation. And so do a dozen highly placed police officers in this town."

"Don't drop names at me, Puma." He glowered and

106

his hands clenched atop the desk.

I said nothing, meeting his glare unflinchingly.

The door opened again, and an officer stuck his head in to say, "Serano's here, Sergeant, with his attorney."

"Send 'em in," Macrae said hoarsely.

Lou Serano came in, saw me and said quickly, "Joe, I didn't put you in a bind, did I?"

"Almost," I said. "Glad you showed, Lou."

Macrae said crisply, "You can go now, Puma. Keep in touch."

"I'd like to wait to see what Mr. Serano has to say," I objected.

A tall, gray-haired man came into the room behind Serano.

Macrae said, "Good-bye, Puma. Keep in touch." He didn't look at me. "Close the door behind you."

I resisted the impulse to slam it. I went out to my car and waited. I had no place special to go and there was a possibility Serano wouldn't be long.

Macrae had been unreasonable. We had worked well together the last time we met and wound up the case as friends. Perhaps he had missed a promotion; he had been a sergeant for a long time.

If he had harbored any real suspicion of me, I wouldn't be sitting in my car; I'd be in a cell. So throwing his weight around had been a low-grade cop attitude and less than I had expected from him.

The death of Brian Delsy was still of official concern to the police, but they had lots of deaths to deal with and each received the approved and efficient mass treatment. Lou and I had a more restricted interest; the other deaths, outside of Tampett's, wouldn't require our attention. Our interest was personal; the Department's official. I sat and waited.

I smoked a cigarette and listened to a platter program on the car radio. I smoked another cigarette without the radio, and then Lou Serano and his attorney came down the steps to the sidewalk.

I got out of the car. Lou saw me and left his lawyer to come over.

He was grinning. "Hot? Going to swing at me?"

I shook my head and smiled. "You came in. Any sensible man would be properly represented before he came in. You tried to get in touch with me this morning through Fidelia. Why?"

"To tell you I'd found out where Tampett was."

"How?"

"I won't ask you how you found out and you won't ask me. Okay?"

"Okay. One other thing—who was the swish who gave you the information on Brian's coming to warn Fidelia?"

He hesitated, looking at me thoughtfully. Then, "All I know is that the boys around Eddie's call him Leslie. I don't know his last name or where he lives."

"And," I said, "——if you want to answer—why did you go to see Tampett?"

"Because I got the word he was covered at the time Delsy died. And if he didn't kill Delsy, maybe, for enough money, he could tell me who did."

"Why do you care who killed Delsy?"

"I don't." He smiled. "Unless, of course, it was Foy. And it could have been."

We stood there quietly a moment. And then I asked, "Who are you working for, Lou? Who's your big-shot friend?"

He chewed his lip. He looked over at his lawyer, who was waiting for him, and back at me. "I—won't tell you, because it's none of your business. But you can tell Fidelia it's the man who tore up the check. *She'll* know."

"Fidelia will tell me," I said.

"Maybe." He lifted a hand. "Take care of yourself, Joe. The road's getting rockier." He went back to join the other man.

When they pulled away, I went back to the Station. Sergeant Macrae was still in the small room and I didn't go there. I found Lieutenant Lusk in his office.

Briefly, I gave him the story leading up to Tampett's death, and then asked, "Has the slug that killed Tampett been found?"

He nodded. "And Sergeant Loepke from Santa Monica has already inquired about it. It's a .38, Joe, but too battered to identify." He paused. "Didn't Sergeant Macrae tell you that?"

"I forgot to ask him," I said. "Anything else I should know, Lieutenant?"

108

"We've got a fingerprint," he said, "but no local identification of it. We're trying Washington."

"And—?"

He shrugged. "And that's it."

Outside, I climbed into the Plymouth again and contemplated my next move. It was four o'clock and I didn't want to go any place that would tangle me with the going-home traffic that was soon to start.

A sense of futility was strong in me. I had had a picture in my mind, the case as I saw it and as I had worded it to Willis Morley. At that time, the flaw in the logical sequence had been the alibi of Robert Tampett, my number-one choice as the killer.

The story was further awry now; the killer was killed.

If his alibi was cracked, he could still be the original killer, but who, then, was guilty of the second murder?

There didn't seem to be any point in leaning on Tampett's neighbors. If the police with all their authority couldn't crack that alibi, it would be reasonable to expect that a man with no authority would have even less luck.

I went home.

I soaked off the bandage on my side and bathed in the tub for a change, slowly and lazily, trying to loosen my tense shoulder muscles, to warm away the ache at the back of my neck.

I was a big nothing getting nowhere. Even at half-pay, Fidelia Sherwood Richards was being cheated. I'd had a case, damn it! A logical, solid, sequential—and impossible—case.

Go back over the route, Punchy Puma, looking for an error or a road fork you missed. Who else but Tampett? Who else? Who, who, who?

Tampett had been a pawn. Had there been others?

After I'd dried myself, I put a fresh pad of gauze on my ribs and sat in the kitchen with a can of beer, thinking back to the beginning, trying to find another route as solid as the one I'd voiced to Willis Morley.

My phone rang. It was Mrs. Foy. "I heard Bob Tampett was killed this afternoon. Is that true?"

"It's true, Mrs. Foy."

There was relief in her voice. "Good. Then I can go home again. I miss that dump."

Good? A man dies and she says "good." I said nothing.

109

"You still there, Puma?"

"I'm here, ma'am. It's safe to go home, now. Good luck."

"Thanks. Remember now, you got a lonely evening, or even afternoon, I got a phone."

"I'll remember." I hung up.

The going-home traffic had thinned out by six o'clock as I drove over to the Avalon Beach, but the beach crowd was still coming in from the west.

Fidelia was in brown and white polished cotton, looking like a college sophomore, cool and innocent, middle-class, adjusted.

"What's wrong?" she asked. "You look weary."

"I am. Bob Tampett's been killed."

She sat motionless, staring at me.

I went over to sit down.

She didn't move. "Do they——do the police know who did it?"

"Nope. Not at four o'clock, they didn't, anyway."

She turned to face me. "Do you?"

"No. Would I be depressed if I did? What kind of question is that?"

"God, you're touchy, aren't you?"

I nodded.

She came over to sit near me. "What's happened, Joe?"

"Two murders, violence and deceit and a big, fat preponderance of self-interest, cynicism, fraudulence and pretense. The same things that always fill my despairing days."

"Maybe you're in the wrong profession."

I said nothing.

"You're quite a bleeder, aren't you?" she asked quietly.

"Tonight, I am." I thought of Mrs. Foy. "There's a lot of loneliness in the world, you know it?"

"Yes, gloomy. Is this a new thought for you? Actually, there isn't much of anything else. Are you going to be depressed all evening?"

"Maybe not. A steak and a couple of beers can do a lot for me. Ready?" I stood up.

She stood up. "I suppose. Smile, Joe Puma. Kiss me gently."

110

I smiled and kissed her on the forehead and we went out to my car.

"We were going down Ocean Front when I asked her, "Do you know a friend of Brian Delsy's named Leslie?"

"Not well. But I know who he is—Les Elkins." A pause. "What did Lou Serano want with you? Did you hear from him?"

"I ran into him over at the house when I found Tampett. I asked him who he was working for and he told me you'd know. It was the man who tore up the check. Does that mean anything to you?"

"It does. He's a—a man I knew in Las Vegas."

"Anybody I know?"

"I doubt it. He's a gambler, I guess. His wife was a patient of Dr. Foy's."

"Serano seems to be checking out clean," I said. "And that eliminates another suspect."

Nothing from her.

The Plymouth rumbled on. One would think we were strangers, or married, the way we sat so quietly and dull. In the west, the sun was burning through the mist beginning to rise from the ocean.

At Eddie's, the boss nodded to us without interest or apparent animosity as we headed for the back corner booth.

The waiter came over and I changed my mind about the beer. I ordered a double bourbon. Fidelia ordered a Manhattan.

That first double jolt accomplished what the hot bath had failed to do; my tensions began to melt. I had two more before our steaks came and the world didn't look nearly as bleak.

We were finished with our steaks and back to the booze when Fidelia said, "Here comes that Leslie Elkins now."

She was facing the doorway. I turned to see a tanned, lean young man with long flaxen hair and brilliant blue eyes. He smiled at Fidelia, looked blankly at me, and headed for a booth at the far end of the room. There was another man with him who was fat and moon-faced.

I excused myself and went over to their booth. Both of them looked up without smiling.

111

"My name is Joe Puma," I said. "Im a private investigator."

"I know," Leslie Elkins said. "We're not in the market for an investigator at the moment, Mr. Puma."

"So run along," the fat boy said.

I looked at him steadily. He looked back at me contemptuously.

I said, "Maybe you haven't heard about my temper, Chubby. I don't want another word out of you." I looked at Elkins. "But I would like to have about a minute of *private* conversation with you."

The fat one muttered something. Elkins said, "Would you go to the bar for a minute, Roy?"

Roy got up grumpily and Elkins watched him go with a smile. Then he looked at me and said, "I suppose you want to talk about Brian?"

"That's right. I understand that you know something about him that the police don't."

"I do. And the police will never learn it from me directly. I have no reason to respect the police in this town, Mr. Puma."

I said nothing. The obvious comment would be embarrassing to both of us.

He said, "I was very close to Brian. I'm going to tell you this, but if you tell the police I was your informant, I'll deny it."

I nodded.

He looked back to see if Fidelia was out of earshot. Then he said, "Brian learned that Dr. Foy and this Morley person—this loan shark—were working together. Dr. Foy thought Morley would be better equipped to handle Fidelia's money; he'd know better how to rob her."

I nodded again, "I suspected as much."

"But then," he went on, "Fidelia became so dependent on Foy, he realized he didn't need Morley. He hoped to marry her. He was sure he could swing it. That was what Brian wanted to tell Fidelia that night he was thrown out of here."

"I'm with you," I said. "It's all solid and it's the way I had it figured. But who killed Brian?"

He shrugged. "That should be easy. Foy's stooge, Bob Tampett."

"Uh-huh. And who, then, killed Tampett?"

112

He stared at me. "Tampett? Bob Tampett? Has he been killed? When?"

"I don't know. I found him this afternoon, dead, in a shack over on Alta Canal."

Elkins' stare widened. "Two-eighteen Alta Canal?"

"That's right. Do you know the house?"

"It belongs to Dr. Foy. Or did. I've been there. That was before he was divorced. When he moved to Beverly Hills, he rented that place to some Mexicans, I remember."

"The police must know that," I mused. "It's strange that they didn't tell me."

"The police," Leslie Elkins said stiffly, "don't confide in anyone but the newspapers. And in the newspapers only when they can destroy someone with filthy publicity."

Again, I didn't comment.

I asked, "Was Tampett your choice for the murderer?"

He nodded.

"He was checked out and clean for the time," I said. "Why not Dr. Foy?"

He shook his head. "Arnold has a temper, quick and furious. But he couldn't maintain his malice long enough for a premeditated murder."

"That's only an opinion," I argued.

"Of course. I guess any of us could kill, if we had to, couldn't we?"

"Almost. Well, Mr. Elkins, thank you. Can you think of anything else that might help? Nobody seems to be mourning poor Mr. Delsy, but I'm determined to find his murderer."

"A lot of people are mourning Brian," he corrected me. "But I can't think of another thing that would help you, Mr. Puma."

When I came back to our booth, Pete Richards was there, talking animatedly with Fidelia.

"You two never should have separated," I said.

Richards smiled. "Yes. we should have. We enjoy each other much more this way."

Fidelia said, "Pete was telling me about your namesake."

I looked at him.

"The guitarist," he explained. "Joe Puma. Haven't you ever heard of him?"

I shook my head.

He sipped his coffee. "About the best in the world, for my money. Real fine. I've a record of his you can have."

From behind the bar, Eddie signalled Pete, and Pete stood up. "My master's voice," he said. "Listen carefully, Fidelia. I'm going to open with another new one."

Her eyes followed him.

When she looked back at me, I said, "He's still *it*, isn't he?"

"No," she said. "It wouldn't work. It didn't work; it wouldn't work." She lifted her empty glass. "More? How about you?"

"More," I said. "Tonight's the night for it."

Chapter Thirteen

Don't get your signals mixed; I'm no boozer. I had worked hard, had come up with the only answer—and had walked into a wall. Frustration was tying me into a psychological knot; I had to unwind.

The bourbon warmed me. The piano of Pete Richards soothed me, leading the mind into channels far from the weary, working world. Across from me, Fidelia sat motionless and entranced.

When Richards finished his first session, he came back to sit with us, bringing a cup of coffee along. He sat next to Fidelia and, though my vision was blurring by this time, I could still see what a fine-looking couple they made.

From what I've seen of marriage, people who belong together never seem to get together. It was a damned shame. In the background, I saw the moon-faced friend of Leslie Elkins sneering at me.

"What are you staring at?" Fidelia asked.

"Leslie Elkins' friend."

She turned around. "You can't see him from where you're sitting. Joe, are you drunk?"

"Not exactly," I said. "I'm—just right. I wish you two would get married again."

114

Pete Richards smiled. "I'm too talented and Fidelia's too rich and beautiful. Don't you worry about us, Joe. We have finally arrived at a perfect working agreement."

A couple of young moderns, and they were so wrong. So right for each other and thinking so wrong. . . . A great one-hundred-proof compassion moved through me and I ordered another drink.

"You Latin lush," Fidelia mocked me. "This is another of your unbridled appetites, is it?"

"Rarely," I said. "I had some knots that needed untying."

"I'll have another one, too," she said.

"And I'll have another cup of coffee," Richards said. . . .

And then the intricate semi-melodies of Pete Richards were coming from the piano again, but Pete still sat across from me, only now with a drink in front of him.

"Time is being telescoped," I told Fidelia.

"I'll bet it is," she said. "What's wrong?"

"Pete sitting next to you and the piano playing. Is it a player piano? Pete shouldn't drink."

"This isn't Pete," she said. "He's at the piano. This is Lou Serano drinking next to me."

I focused my eyes carefully, but it looked like the moon-faced man to me.

Lou's voice came from the moon-face. "Cheers, Joe! What's new?"

"My guitar," I said. "Where's Foy? Foy should be here."

Lou laughed. "We could stick him with the check."

"Let's get off the Foy kick," Fidelia said.

"I will if you will," I told her. "Let us here and now take a solemn pledge, the three of us, to give up Foy."

Nobody answered me.

"We're either brothers or we're not," I insisted. "This is the test, brothers."

"I'm not a brother," Fidelia said. "And you wouldn't want me for a sister. You'd worry. You'd worry all the time. I'd never have any dates; you'd chase them all away."

In my addled mind, something triggered a response and I reached for it—and it slipped away, intangible as smoke.

115

The piano moved into a new tune, and Fidelia finished her drink and stood up. "Pardon me. Don't go away, boys; I'll be back."

Lou's face came into focus. "I didn't want to say anything, Joe, while she was sitting here, but the police have taken Dr. Foy into temporary custody."

"Good," I said.

"Maybe. But don't say anything to Fidelia, will you? We don't know if she's cured of Foy."

"She's cured," I said. "To hell with Foy. You should meet his wife, Lou, and let her tell you about Dr. Arnold Foy, graduate of the Sunset College of Clinical Psychology."

"The Kunket Sollege?" he said. "What's that?"

"You heard me, Lou. Don't give me any trouble."

Fidelia's voice. "Here we go again! Now, what's the rub? You live in a state of constant indignation, don't you?"

"Welcome home," I said. "Where have you been?"

I don't know what she answered; there was a blank here, longer than the others.

When cognizance returned, the moon-face was there again, complete with sneer.

"You're not kidding me with that mask, Serano," I said. "I know your voice."

"How bright of you," the moon-face said, and it wasn't Serano's voice.

And there was another face next to the moon-face now. It wasn't Leslie Elkins', though it was just as thin and petulant. And next to that face there was still another and I looked around for Fidelia, for Richards and his piano, for Lou Serano and Eddie.

All I could find around me was the night. And a dim light coming through a window and reflecting off a wall not six feet away. I had the damnedest feeling that I was in an alley, but that couldn't be. How would I get into an alley?

"Tough guy," Moon-face said. "Inside, you were so mouthy. Why so quiet now?"

"You got me, chubby," I said. "I just feel quiet, I guess. Where am I? I got this silly feeling I'm in an alley. What would I do in an alley?"

116

Moon-face chuckled. "Fight or fall, that's what you'll do in this alley. Or fight *and* fall. Or maybe just fall?"

"Fight?" I said. "That's okay. I like to fight. But are we mad at each other? You should tell me that so I know how to fight, full strength or half."

"Fight full strength," the man with the petulant face said. "We want to take you at your best."

I forced my eyes to focus and they focused on the moon-face. I spread my feet a little and smiled—and threw the first big punch at the middle of the moon.

That, I think, was my best punch of the night. Because I could feel the cartilage go in his nose and a tooth snap on the left side of his mouth. Considering all the life-giving bourbon I was loaded with, I'm surprised now his neck didn't break.

Someone hit me a trivial blow in the side, and I backhanded lustily and accurately—because that someone yelped. And was someone else crying? Someone was whimpering. I hoped it was old moon-face.

Wham! One of them could hit. The punch missed my chin but caught my throat and I fought for breath, searching the darkness desperately for the next one.

It came, high on the chin this time, and I went back into a rough stucco wall, and started to go down. What was I doing, fighting with my fists like a lousy amateur boxer? As I started to go down, I threw the right foot straight out in front of me, my back firmly anchored by the wall.

It had to be a groin I caught. Because the sickening grunt and the piteous moan that followed contact came from a throat too weak for a sound to match the pain.

And now there were two whimpers, the sad cries of broken men, too badly hurt to be shamed by their tears.

And in my right hand there was a throat and above the throat there was the face as thin as Leslie Elkins' that didn't belong to Leslie Elkins. And I could feel my forearm muscles tightening and the pull of them going into my bicep muscles. And the big shoulder muscles were coming into action. . . .

When, from the ground, someone said hoarsely, "Puma, you're killing him! Let go, please let go of him! Please, please, please!"

I was killing him. And I say this right now, honestly —I'm not sure I would have quit squeezing if I hadn't heard the siren. I was drunk—dead, stinking drunk—and full of the day's rage.

But the siren was loud and close, so I dropped him. I looked toward the light at the open end of the alley and knew I couldn't go out that way.

I turned, hoping to hell it wasn't a dead-end alley.

I took about five steps, and walked into a wall. It was a dead-end.

Desperately, I turned back, but there was the squeal of braking tires at the curb in front now. My only exit was blocked.

And then my hand felt a doorknob and I held my breath. The doorknob turned, the door opened—and I stepped into a dimly lighted washroom. I expelled my breath and locked the door behind me.

Through the other door, I could hear the sound of a piano and it was Pete Richards' piano. I was finding my point in time and space.

In the mirror above the sink, I could see my face; it was bruised but not bloody. In the mirror above the sink, I could see the whole damned washroom and my grievous error.

Some important plumbing equipment was missing for me. It was the ladies' washroom.

Cautiously, I opened the door and looked out. There was only a small screen disguising this door, and a woman stood at the end of it, talking to Eddie. I closed it again and headed for the only sanctuary in sight, the room's single cubicle.

I went in and sat down.

If my victims squealed to the police, now out in front, the police would come looking for me. I smiled. They would look every place.

Every place but *here*.

I was surrounded by sheet steel and there was a sliding bolt lock on the sheet steel door in front of me. Great stuff, steel. Great protector of the innocent, guardian of the oppressed.

Only when the hubbub in front died down would I leave this handy sanctuary.

I heard the door open and some footsteps come in. I heard a feminine voice ask, "What's all the fuss about?"

And another feminine voice answered, "I don't know. Some kind of trouble outside. A fight, I guess. Eddie says the law is looking for that big man who was in here with the Sherwood dame."

"Joe Puma, you mean?"

"That's the name—Puma."

"I hope they don't find him," the other voice said. "I wish I could find him first. What a man, huh?"

"I guess. I don't go much for them foreign types."

"Honey, you need glasses. Yum, yum, yummy!"

"Glasses I don't need," the other voice said. "Just some light in this dump. The business Eddie is doing on that Richards, you'd think he'd splurge on a big bulb for the johnny. How do I look?"

"Thirty-three and badly used," my admirer answered. "Is that growler occupied or did Eddie lock it up again?" There was a rap on the steel door in front of me. "Anybody in there?"

I leaned over and rapped back.

"You sick, honey? Can't you talk?"

I rapped back again.

"Hey," my admirer said worriedly, "I'll bet this dame is over the edge. Maybe she needs help. You'd better tell Eddie, huh?"

I took a breath and said in my sweetest falsetto, "I'm all right. It won't be long now."

A long, long silence. And then my non-admirer said, "If that's a dame in there, I'm Gregory Peck."

My admirer said quickly, "You're damned right it's a dame. If you want to break up a seven-year friendship, Genevieve Pelson, go ahead. If you don't, that's a girl in there; a sweet, friendly girl."

Genevieve said, "Dorothy, you're insane!"

"Like a fox," Dorothy said. "Genevieve Pelson, if—"

There was a knock on the door leading to the bar—and silence. And then a muffled voice that sounded like Eddie's. "Girls, you all right? Would you check that place for the police? They're looking for Puma."

"There's no Puma in here," Dorothy said, "unless she's hiding in the drain."

119

"It's not a *she,* it's a *he,*" Eddie said. "The private investigator, Joe Puma."

Then Genevieve put in her nickel's worth. "We'll look again, Eddie, though with this bulb you got in here, it's hard to see *anything."* Some shuffling of feet. "Nobody here but us chickens, Eddie."

Silence.

Relief flooded through me and the haziness came back.

One little vignette stands out in my memory, though I couldn't swear to it. Somebody passed a drink under the door and I drank it.

A face came into my vision again. The face was Fidelia's, but the voice wasn't. The voice was Mona Greene's.

"Lover," the voice said. "Strong, gentle lover."

I reached for the body with the face of Fidelia and the voice of Mona Greene. The breasts were full, but there was some sag to them. Was this the body of Mrs. Foy?

Only in the breasts was there any sag; the legs were firm and long, the tummy taut. In the moonlight coming through the window, I could see the whiteness that had been covered by a bathing suit.

She chuckled. "Jen should see me now."

"Who's Jen?" I asked.

"My girl friend. Genevieve Pelson. Don't you remember? I room with her. That's why we came here?"

"Where is *here?"*

"At your friend's apartment. Don't you remember? You said you couldn't go home, so your friend brought you here. And you insisted I come along."

"Now I remember," I said. "Genevieve is the one who doesn't go much for foreign types. I'll bet you're Dorothy." I paused. "The cute one."

A silence. With women, a silence so often means trouble, trouble, trouble. . . .

A sniff. "I like that. You aren't that drunk, Joe Puma. I like *that!* What do you think I am, some tramp or something?"

I put a hand on her tight tummy. "No, no, no. You're darling Dorothy. You saved my neck."

"That's better," she said, mollified. "I felt like kind of

120

a tramp, your friend sleeping in the other room and all —putting him in the living room, I mean. I guess he's . . . modern, though, isn't he?"

"He sure is," I agreed. Which friend, which friend? I didn't have the courage to ask her. I whispered, "Don't you think he's a great guy?"

"I guess. I don't know him well. He sure plays my kind of piano, though."

That friend. I put a hand in her hair. It was soft and clean and fragrant. I moved closer.

"Again?" she whispered. "You're some man!"

Again? I had missed one. Or more? That's a hell of a thing to miss.

"Who counts?" I said. "Do you count, darling Dorothy?"

"Not with you," she said. "It's always the first time, with you."

Darling Dorothy. I pulled her close, wondering what she'd look like in the morning.

Chapter Fourteen

In the morning, she wasn't there. An unclouded sun poured through the unshaded window and I was wet with perspiration. The odor of Dorothy's perfume was still faintly in the room. Through the door came the soft sound of Richards' piano.

The bathroom was off this bedroom; I showered before going out. From the piano, Richards looked over and smiled. "Alone?"

"It seems that way. How did I get here last night?"

"I drove your car. You weren't in any shape to drive it. And you figured the law would be waiting for you at your place."

On a sofa against the far wall of the room, a sheet and two blankets were folded. "You gave us your bed," I said.

"Why not? You like eggs?" He stood up. "Toast, orange juice or tomato juice, Wheaties."

"Eggs, thanks," I said. "What time is it?"

121

"Around ten. How about some baking soda and water?"

"Just a couple aspirin, if you have 'em."

He smiled wryly. "I've got a million I'll never need again. In the bathroom. How many eggs, Joe?"

I said humbly, "Don't flinch, but I usually have six."

He went to the kitchen and I went after the aspirin. When I came into the kitchen there was a cup of coffee waiting for me, and the *Times*.

The *Times* had the story on Dr. Foy, but he had been released after a short questioning. The paper didn't have the story of my alley brawl. Nor anything new on the first murder; simply a tired rehash and various pronouncements by politically-minded officials. Tampett's murder had stirred the papers, who were now stirring the people, making the politicians restless.

At the stove, Pete Richards put a huge, rectangular aluminum griddle over two of the burners. "Sunny-side up?" he asked.

"Right. Who took Fidelia home last night?"

"Eddie. She stayed until closing."

"What happened to Lou Serano?"

"I don't know. He wasn't there when we closed the joint." He turned around. "How did you get into the alley with those drips?"

I shrugged. "The whole night's full of blanks for me. But this I remember, what a fine couple you and Fidelia make."

"Get off that, please?" he asked quietly. "There are reasons; I mean——" He expelled his breath irritatedly. "I wish you wouldn't talk about it in front of Fidelia. It's—embarrassing." He turned back to the sizzling eggs.

I said nothing. Embarrassing? Why? I continued to say nothing. The smell of eggs and butter filled my nostrils, making my impatient stomach growl.

He put some toast into the toaster and came over to slide six white and golden eggs onto an enormous plate. He sat down across from me with two fried eggs of his own.

The silence continued through three of my eggs. And then I said, "I don't understand that. About it being embarrassing, I mean."

He took a deep breath and looked at me with great

122

patience. "Joe, I gave you, and your friend, lodging for the night, after driving you here, keeping you out of jail. And then I cook you six eggs. Now, all I ask in return is, don't pry!"

"I'm sorry," I said. "These are fine eggs."

He ate quietly, his head down. He'd been genial enough before breakfast; I must have hit a nerve. I read the theatrical news in the *Times* while he read the sports pages. You'd think we were married, the way we ignored each other.

He was in the right, of course. He had harbored me in a bad time and I had badgered him. I finished the theatrical news and poured myself another cup of coffee. He poured his second cup and lit a cigarette. He looked around the room and his eyes met mine. He looked away.

"Thanks," I said, "for everything."

"It's okay," he said. "Sorry if I seemed to get miffed about nothing. I suppose you'd better check in at the Venice Station. Will you have to tell them I hid you for the night?"

"No. I'll run over there now and get cleared away." I stood up. "What's that Dorothy's last name?"

He shrugged. "I don't know. Why? Did you plan to send her a bill?"

What I planned to send her was some flowers, but I didn't voice this. I didn't want him to think of me as sentimental. I thanked him again and went out into a blazing near-noon sun.

In last night's alcoholic haze some incident or remark had almost triggered a hunch that might have led to a new line of inquiry, but it was lost in this morning's sobriety. The picture still showed me Tampett as the key piece and Tampett was now beyond mortal inquiry.

So, I told myself, it's always darkest just before dawn.

In this optimistic spirit, I entered the small room at the Venice Station where Sergeant Macrae was making out some reports.

He looked up and his sour Scots face turned even more sour. "Start lying," he said.

I stared at him in innocent surprise. "What about? I understand I was being looked for last night, so I came in to make myself available."

123

"One of those boys," he said grimly, "was released from the hospital only an hour ago. So start lying."

I sat down in a nearby chair. "I went there to talk with a man named Leslie Elkins. He had some information on Delsy. Evidently, Elkins', well, *good friend,* resented my interest in sweet Leslie. So he chose me. He didn't want to tackle me alone; he brought two friends along. So they dragged me out into the alley—and whammo!"

"Sure," he said cynically. "There were three of them; that much we have to admit. So it puts you about half-way out of trouble."

"How do I work out the other half, Sergeant?" I asked humbly.

"You answer two questions," he said.

I sat back and nodded.

"First," he said, "how did you get away from the officers?"

"I hid out in the ladies' john."

His chin came up and he half-smiled. "You're kidding."

I shook my head. "Next question?"

He said musingly, "I'd like to ask what conversations you may have overheard in there. I've often wondered what women talk about when——" He broke off.

"Sergeant," I said warmly, "you're almost human."

He cleared his throat. "Second question. Tell me all you know about this Delsy-Tampett murder. *Including your theories.*"

I worded it to him as I had to Willis Morley. And finished by saying, "Then Tampett is killed—and everything goes out the window."

"Not completely," he corrected me. "There's an answer in there, somewhere. We've got that ballistics report that pins the gun on Tampett. He shot you with it."

I said nothing.

"Foy," he went on, "is clean. We sweated him yesterday. So who next? Morley?"

"I have no idea, Sergeant. I'm really nowhere. I had it all sewed up—and a stitch came loose."

"A stitch, sure, but the whole damned thing didn't unravel. You've done some fine work here, Joe. You can't quit now."

"Why can't I? Who appreciates me? Do you? Look how you treated me last time I was in here."

"Cut it out," he said. "A big slob like you, sulking. It's enough to turn my stomach. You're getting paid, aren't you?"

"*Half* my usual fee," I answered.

"One way or another, you're getting paid," he said caustically. He leaned back. "How about Mrs. Fidelia Sherwood Richards? What's her alibi for the night Delsy was killed?"

A real long silence. He smiled at me and I glared at him. Finally, I said, "Ask her."

He continued to smile. "As soon as I've called the reporters. They're entitled to hear it. The press in this town has a great interest in the Sherwood adventures."

I was breathing heavily.

"I'm glad I'm in the Department," he said. "You wouldn't hit a police officer, would you, Investigator Puma?"

"I have," I said. "Only the other day in Santa Monica, I popped one." I shrugged my shoulder muscles, trying to relieve the tension at the base of my neck. "Considering my reputation, I think I get pretty damned lousy treatment from the Los Angeles Police Department."

He smiled. "You wouldn't want it any other way. If people started to be nice to you, it would destroy you."

"Don't butter me, Sergeant. It's out of character." I stood up. "Did those boys I fought file any charges?"

"They've withdrawn them," he said, and paused. "After I talked with them this morning."

"Well!" I studied him. "Maybe I've got friends I don't even know about."

"I wouldn't be a damned bit surprised," he admitted. "You're quite a man. Carry on, you slob."

He was all right, that Sergeant Macrae. The city was damned lucky to have him at the starvation prices it paid. Teachers and cops, the only two trades our civilization absolutely has to have. And we pay them peanuts.

The sun was still boiling in a cloudless sky. Perspiration ran down my sides and my wound itched under the bandage.

In the grounds of the Avalon Beach, the big palms

125

afforded shade and the breeze coming over the clay bluffs above the ocean was cooling.

The breeze wasn't as cool as Mrs. Fidelia Sherwood Richards' welcome. She opened the door of her cottage and glared at me.

"I'm not free-loading," I explained. "I've already eaten a big breakfast."

"It's lunchtime, now."

"I had a late breakfast, with your recent husband. He took care of me last night after you deserted me."

"Huh!" she said.

"Do we stand here and bicker for the neighbors," I asked, "or do I come in?"

"Come in," she said. "Come in and start lying, you vulgar, loud——"

"Sergeant Macrae told me the same thing. Where did you and Eddie wind up?"

"Home," she said furiously. "Right here!"

I raised my eyebrows. "You and Eddie? Fidelia, he's a married man."

"He brought me here and left me," she said icily. "Don't try to change the subject. Don't you think I don't know dear old Pete was trying to hide that—that *tramp* from me. You went with her, didn't you? You're probably diseased, right now."

"What tramp?" I asked innocently. "You don't mean some *girl,* do you?"

"Girl? I mean that weather-beaten, bar-battered, whiskey-voiced, stilt-legged——" She took a deep breath.

"Fidelia," I said gently, "phone Pete right now. This second. Please? Ask him about me."

"Why should I phone him? I know the girl went with Pete. And you've just told me you went with Pete. So who in the hell would the girl be with?"

I chewed my lower lip and studied the ceiling thoughtfully. "Let's see, now. Why, the girl would be with Pete, natch. She went with him, right?"

"And what would Pete Richards want with a girl?"

"Fidelia, it's none of your business. Are you jealous?"

"I'm asking you, Joseph Puma, as calmly as I can, what would *impotent* Pete Richards want with a girl?"

That was what he meant when he said I was embar-

126

rassing him. That was why he and Fidelia were divorced. I stared at her and said, "That's what he meant!"

"That is what *who* meant?"

"Pete," I answered. "May I sit down? It's a mixed-up story."

She nodded grimly.

I sat down and stared thoughtfully at the floor. I looked up at her and said earnestly, "I can't tell you much about last night. I dimly remember a girl coming with us to Pete's. And then, some time in the night, I woke up and heard this horrible argument going on between Pete and a girl. I suppose it was the girl who came with us. She called him some names I don't want to repeat." I shook my head. "It was pretty sickening. This morning, when I asked Pete what the fight was all about, he seemed embarrassed. When I pressed him, just for gags, he told me quite plainly that any further discussion along those lines would embarrass him, and I should shut my mouth."

Fidelia sat down across from me, staring doubtfully.

"And now you tell me," I said. "He's impotent, huh? That's why you got divorced?"

She continued to stare at me doubtfully. "If you're lying, you're good at it. But you would be. Lying well is important in your profession, isn't it?"

Only in my love life, I thought. I said, "I don't lie any more than anyone else, and never to clients."

"Even half-price clients? I suppose I'm only entitled to half the truth from you."

"Fidelia, be reasonable. Did I make a fuss about your coming home with a married man?"

"You're being absurd," she said.

"And you're not? Think of who you are and who I am and you'll realize, I'm sure, that your tantrum was adolescent."

"Who I am?" She wrinkled her forehead. "Class conscious, are you?"

"Always," I said. "Most poor people are."

"It's a form of snobbery, isn't it? It's inverted snobbery."

"Probably," I agreed. "You're still in love with Pete, aren't you?"

She shook her head.

127

"And he with you," I went on. "I see now why you two don't fight."

She looked dully past me at nothing. She seemed spent, emotionally exhausted.

"You need a comeback drink," I said. "You were really belting that booze, last night."

"*I* was? How about you, Gargantua?"

"We both need a drink," I agreed. "Some hair of the dog. You phone, and I'll buy."

She picked up the phone and called for room service. She ordered bourbon, replaced the phone on its cradle and looked at me sadly.

I winked at her.

"I was adolescent, wasn't I?" she said. "We're not married. What difference should it make to me what you did last night?"

I sighed and leaned back, rubbing my neck.

"After all," she went on, "in a sense, you're really only an employee, aren't you?"

I nodded.

"And I knew your reputation, long before I met you."

"Right," I said. "Feeling better now?"

"Not a bit," she said. "You damned tomcat!"

Chapter Fifteen

There is no point in trying to reason with a woman. They don't operate from the intellect but are wired directly to their emotions, and reason is wasted on them.

Fidelia had a drink and felt better. We talked quietly, avoiding any reference to last night. Though the talk was quiet, it was strained and unnatural; she was obviously itching to tell me off again.

And why? We were not children. Such fleshly alliance as we had enjoyed was doomed to be temporary; it established no proprietary rights. Of course, I had taken her to Eddie's and not been available for return transportation. But that was only a social oversight and slim excuse for her possessive fury.

128

She finished her drink and sat quietly in her chair.

I finished my drink and stood up. "I'm wasting your money, Fidelia. I thought I had it, but I don't. I'm nowhere."

"Finish the day," she said wearily. "The other money is already spent."

"Other money?"

She didn't look at me. "The money you've charged me so far."

Annoyance stirred in me. It wasn't the first indication of her penuriousness. I held my tongue. She was getting cut-rate service already, but I held my tongue. I thought of the man at Vegas who had torn up the check. Maybe she was a bad loser, too.

She looked up. "Don't voice what you're thinking."

"I won't. Do you want me to quit now? I won't charge you for today."

"Finish the day," she said. "Then send your bill to my attorneys. Gallegher, Hartford and Leedom, in Beverly Hills."

"Okay," I said, and started for the door, waiting for her to call me back. She didn't call, and I paused at the door, giving her a final chance.

She wasn't even looking at me; I went out.

From near-hysteria to despondency in half an hour. Well, maybe she had run down. Maybe her stamina had been depleted by last night's excitement and not left her enough energy to sustain her rage.

Or maybe a thought had struck her.

My peasant's intuition was rumbling in me, begging to be heard. It wasn't the eggs. It was a hunch trying to be born.

In that fluster of angry words, some hint of truth had come through to her and made her rage meaningless. It couldn't have been the drink; one drink couldn't make her that quiet. I thought back to our first night together and remembered how soundly I had slept. Had she seen something while I was asleep? Had she seen Brian Delsy die?

From a lobby phone, I called Sergeant Macrae at the Venice Station. "On that fingerprint," I asked him. "How soon would you expect an answer?"

"Tomorrow, maybe. Why?"

"I just wondered. If the guy had been in the service, his fingerprints would be on file in Washington, wouldn't they?"

"Yup. Come on, Puma—let us in on your hunches."

"I haven't any. One's trying to be born. So help me, that's the solemn truth."

A pause, and then he said, "Okay, Joe. Carry on."

In the phone book, I found the number of Leslie Elkins and called that, hoping to find him at home.

I did. I said, "Joe Puma. Could I talk with you today? I'm right in the neighborhood."

"I suppose. About Brian?"

"That's right. Your . . . friends aren't around, are they?"

"Friends?" he asked. Then, "Oh, those roughnecks who attacked you? They're no longer friends of mine, Mr. Puma."

"Glad to hear it," I said. "They're a rowdy bunch. I'll be over in a few minutes."

Geographically, it wasn't much of a trip from the Avalon Beach to Leslie Elkins' three-room house on a back lot off Ludlow Street. But it was a long step down in property values.

It was a small frame house, leaning and obviously ancient, though freshly painted. Leslie Elkins was waiting for me at the front door.

Inside, he had covered the walls with a rough fabric similar to monk's cloth and decorated in silver grays and soft pastels, with an occasional ebony accent. It was peaceful and cool and in impeccable taste.

I looked around and said, "This makes me thoroughly ashamed of my little ratrap. But what can a man do, lacking taste?"

He smiled. "Would you like something cool to drink? How about a gin and tonic?"

"I'd like one, thank you." I sat on a low love seat and looked out at his small, fenced garden full of flowers.

He mixed a pair of drinks and brought me one. He sat in a low, ultra-modern chair close by and lifted his drink. "To better understanding."

We drank.

Then I said, "You told me last night that you were a very good friend of Brian Delsy's."

He nodded without looking at me. "I was."

"Despite that," I went on, "I hope you can look back at his temperament, his . . . disposition objectively and also understand that honest answers from you could lead to the discovery of his murderer."

He nodded once more, looking up to meet my gaze.

"Was he," I asked quietly, "in any sense malicious or unkind?"

A pause. Then Leslie Elkins nodded for the third time. "He could be. He had a streak of cruelty, of arrogance, in him." He smiled wanly. "I'm sure you have reason to remember his arrogance."

"I do. Think carefully now. Would it be possible that Mr. Delsy wanted to warn Mrs. Richards about Dr. Foy out of some malicious intent?"

Leslie Elkins took a shallow sip of his drink and a deep breath. He said very softly, "It is entirely possible. Brian was not helped by Dr. Foy. Fidelia was. It's not a nice thing to say about a dead man, but Brian might have resented Fidelia's cure."

"Cure?" I said. "It wasn't that, was it? She became almost totally dependent on Dr. Foy."

"She did. But he helped her in other ways. You see, with Fidelia hanging onto Foy for her continued, well, adjustment, Brian was playing with fire when he tried to degrade Foy's image in her mind."

"This arrogance of Delsey's, this streak of cruelty— was it commonly know?"

Leslie Elkins frowned. "Commonly? That's too broad a word. To his intimates, yes. To the boys who drink at Eddie's."

"Did Lou Serano know it?"

"I doubt it. I'm sure Bob Tampett did, though. Who could have killed Tampett?"

"The same person who killed Delsy," I said. "Probably. They were allied deaths, one way or another." I finished my drink and stood up.

Leslie Elkins said, "You're groping, aren't you? You're working on some intuition that you can't even define?"

"That's right. How could you tell?"

He smiled dimly. "I've been called a number of things in this vulgar world, Mr. Puma, but nobody has ever called me insensitive."

"You're quite a guy," I said. "I mean that as a compliment."

"So are you," he answered. "Though I'm not sure I mean it as a compliment. Have I helped?"

"I think you have. I have to start the wheels turning again before I get a pattern, but it will come. Thank you for the drink and the information, Mr. Elkins."

"I hope I've helped," he said softly. "I miss Brian."

I went out into the ugly world again and drove to the office. The mail was all third class and my answering service had no messages. I sat near a window and looked down at the traffic below.

The old pattern re-formed, pointing to Tampett. The gun, the shill, the steerer, Robert Tampett, deceased.

My phone rang, startling me.

It was Fidelia. "What are you doing?"

"Thinking."

"I . . . was unreasonable, wasn't I?"

"Women are. You wouldn't want to be anything but a woman, would you?"

"Not when you're around. Joe, quit. I can guess what you're sitting there thinking about, but where can it lead? Who will be helped if you go on?"

"Justice," I said. "The law."

"Technically only. Two unpleasant people are dead. Was either of them any loss to the world?"

"I don't know. I'm not a judge. And neither are you, Fidelia."

A silence, and then, "I suppose you'd be angry if I —if I talked about money, about paying you to quit, right now?"

"I'm not angry. The answer is no, Fidelia. I'm no saint, but I still live on the saints' side of the street."

"If you go on," she said, "you'll never see me again. I suppose that doesn't bother you."

"It bothers me. You must realize I'm not enjoying my thoughts at the moment. I'm no lamb-stalker, but the law is the law. I've cut some cute corners for fast dollars, but there's a line I walk, just the same."

"You'll send me back to Foy," she said. "Is that what you want?"

"No. You hired me, remember. I wouldn't have gone on this hunt if you hadn't hired me to."

Silence. Then, "Did you have to say that?"

I didn't answer.

In a moment, I heard the click of a closed line. She had hung up.

Last night she had said, "And you wouldn't want me for a sister." I would. If I couldn't have her as a lover, a friend or a sister, even an in-law would be okay. I loved Fidelia. Everybody who had any sense loved Fidelia.

I went down to the car and headed for Santa Monica.

Chapter Sixteen

He wasn't in the yard, soaking up the sun, this afternoon. I climbed the outside stairs to the second-floor apartment, on the runway overlooking the court.

He opened the door to my ring and smiled at me. "More eggs?"

"Nope," I said. "Business, Pete."

He looked at me appraisingly a moment and then opened the door wider. "Come in."

I came in and he closed the door behind me. He went over to sit on the piano bench; I sat in a rattan chair nearby. He leaned forward on the bench, his back to the piano, staring at me.

"I had it all figured," I said, "right to Tampett. It was the only way it made sense. And it made sense, up to him."

The phone rang and he looked up quickly, startled as I had been in my office. He looked at me.

"Answer it," I said.

He stood up, went to the phone and said, "Hello."

A pause, and he said, "I can't run. Where can I run to? Can I run away from myself?" A pause. "Anyway, it's too late. He's here." A pause. "Calm down. Please. Yes, yes, I'll phone back." He hung up.

He came back to take the same position on the piano bench, leaning forward, his eyes fastened on me.

"Was that Fidelia on the phone?" I asked him.

He shook his head.

"Yes, it was, Pete. She phoned before and told you to run away, didn't she?"

He shook his head again. "Get on with your story, Joe."

"It made sense all the way to Tampett," I repeated, "who was a stooge for Foy. But Tampett found himself another stooge, didn't he? Why didn't you admit the other day that when Tampett and Serano sat together in that booth, you were sitting with them?"

"I was drunk," he said. "I didn't remember sitting with them?"

"Tampett found a new stooge," I went on. "A man so drunk he almost didn't know what he was doing. He convinced this man, *you*, that Brian's story on Foy would unhinge Fidelia, might possibly destroy her. And you were drunk enough to go along with the idea, weren't you?"

Richards stared at the floor.

"Tampett gave you the gun," I continued. "You thought you were helping Fidelia.

He said nothing.

"Am I right?" I asked quietly.

He looked up. "You could be, Joe. Only remember I was stinking drunk. That's no excuse to give a jury, I know, but you're not a jury. And I'm going to tell you something you didn't know—Foy did help Fidelia. I lied to you before. Fidelia was an addict. Morphine, Joe. And Foy helped her to break the habit."

I stared at him, only half believing.

"So help me," he said fervently, "it's the gospel truth. And that night, when Tampett got to me with his story, I was so stinking drunk I didn't know right from wrong."

"That night you were drunk. But you weren't drunk when you killed Tampett. Did Tampett try to blackmail you?"

Richards nodded. "He tried. But I didn't kill him. I swear to you I had nothing to do with Tampett's death." He took a hoarse, shallow breath. "And I still don't be-

134

lieve I killed Delsy." He rubbed his throat. "Though I can't be sure. It was a nightmare."

"Where's the gun?" I asked him. "You must have the gun."

He shook his head. "I brought it back to Tampett. That much I remember. He gave me the gun and conned me about Delsy and how he had to be killed. And then there's the drunken nightmare and all I remember is bringing the gun back to Tampett."

"Had you ever shot a gun before?"

He shook his head.

"And you were blind drunk?"

He raised a hand. "I swear it."

"Then how in hell did you get from Eddie's to the Avalon Beach? You sure as hell didn't walk it and you were in no shape to drive."

"Tampett drove me, I suppose," he said.

"Tampett? A little while ago you said you remember *bringing* the gun back to Tampett. If he was with you, you wouldn't be bringing the gun back; he'd be there."

His eyes narrowed. "Somebody drove me. I know *somebody* drove me, because we went around one turn kind of fast and my stomach almost gave out. I remember that. Damn it, I kept thinking of him as Tampett, but it couldn't have been, could it? He was alibied for the time."

I nodded—and his doorbell rang. He looked at the door and at me. I nodded again, and he rose and went to the door.

It was Fidelia. She and Pete went over to sit on the piano bench. I sat down again in the same chair.

"Well?" she said.

I said nothing, trying to think.

"Money, Joe," she said. "Money, money, money—"

"Maybe we're both wrong, Fidelia," I told her. "Maybe Pete is innocent."

"I know I didn't kill Tampett," he said quietly. "And I can't believe, drunk or sober, that I could kill *anybody*."

"I can't either," Fidelia said. She looked at me hopefully.

"Money," I said. "Nobody kills for loyalty, do they? For love or money, for hate or bigotry, they kill." I took

135

a breath. "Have you been living on your income lately?"

She stared at me, perplexed. "On my allowance? Yes, strangely enough, I have."

"All right," I said. "Now would be the time to tell me the name of the man in Las Veges who tore up the check."

"Don Ranzio," she said. "He runs the Yucca Inn."

"Was his wife a patient of Dr. Foy's?"

"Briefly. Why?"

I went to the phone and called the Yucca Inn in Las Vegas. I was in luck; Don Ranzio was in and he had heard of me. He told me what I wanted to know.

I came back to sit across from them again. I held Fidelia's gaze and asked her gently, "How long were you on it?"

Her chin lifted and she colored.

"It's no time to be maidenly," I warned her. "How long were you on it and what was it costing you?"

"Does it matter how long I was on it? It cost me well over forty thousand dollars, the price I was paying for it. I only had one source, and I was paying *his* price."

"One source," I said. "Lou Serano?"

She didn't answer. She looked at her hands in her lap.

Pete Richards said, "The price she was paying, it could have cost her the wad, eventually."

Fidelia looked at him and said softly, "So *you* told him, did you? Why, Pete?"

He didn't look at her. "Because it might be a lead. Because I don't want to go to the gas chamber."

Again, Fidelia looked hopefully at me.

"It's out in left field," I said. "Maybe it can't even be forced into a pattern. But there's an alliance involved I'd like to connect. All we have is a fingerprint down at the Venice Station and it's not Lou Serano's."

"Lou Serano was sitting in the booth that night," Richards said. "I always had the feeling he was working with Tampett."

"Lou works with anyone who can help him," I explained, "and when the person can no longer help him, he works alone. This much I learned from my phone call —Lou wasn't working for Don Ranzio."

There was a silence.

Again, I looked at Fidelia. "Another question. Did

Brian Delsy know you had been on morphine and that Serano was your supplier?"

She nodded and didn't look at me.

"Foy and Tampett," I explained, "was one connection we uncovered. I should have looked further. Because there was another alliance, with more to gain." And I thought, *money, money, money—it's always love or money.* I asked Richards, "Would you risk your neck if it might save you from the gas chamber?"

"Hell, yes," he said.

So we set it up. It was still a Santa Monica deal, so I went down to talk with Sergeant Loepke and Mel Braun. Loepke didn't like it.

"We have procedures," he said. "We can't get tricky. We're *police* officers, Puma."

"Okay," I said wearily. "How about letting the West Los Angeles boys in to work with me, then? Or the boys from the Venice Station?"

He drew himself up haughtily. "We handle our own affairs in Santa Monica. We don't need outside help."

"I do, Sergeant. Lieutenant Lusk, at the Venice Station, has a fingerprint he hasn't matched up. We might need it."

"If we need it, we'll get it." He took a deep breath. "All right, let's have the name of your suspect."

I shook my head. "If you won't work my way, Sergeant, I'm not working with you."

He sat there, glaring at me.

Mel Braun said quietly, "I'll work with him, Sergeant. You won't need to be involved. And I'm sure Locker will work with me. Puma's right on this one; standard police procedure won't do it."

Sergeant Loepke's face was immobile, his jawline tense.

I said, "Remember the talk we had at my place? I'm for *any* procedure that brings criminals to justice, Sergeant. If that's dishonest, then I am, and I don't give a damn. I hate killers."

Sergeant Loepke got up and went over to the water cooler. He drank three paper cups full of water, crumpled the cup in his hand and threw it at the waste basket.

"Damn these kind of shenanigans," he said gruffly.

"Sergeant," I said, "you fight evil any way you can lick it."

He shook his head. "That's not true. But go ahead. I'll stay here until I hear from you. I'm an hour past quitting time right now, but I'll stay here to sweat 'em, if you're lucky."

It was in the most exclusive area of Santa Monica, on San Vicente Boulevard. I parked a couple of blocks away, on a side street. I didn't want Serano to know I was with Richards, if Serano wasn't already there.

It was a fairly large house, hidden from the boulevard by a tall hedge behind a fieldstone wall. There were two cars in the parking area near the garage, but neither of them was a black Caddy convertible.

"Wait here," I said to Richards, and went along under the shadow of the overhang to the side door of the garage.

It was unlocked, and I opened it. My pencil flash showed me the Cad convertible. Lou Serano had hidden his car, too. And perhaps he wouldn't be visible in the house.

I came back to Richards and we went up to the front door together. Our host opened the door only seconds after we had rung his bell.

He peered out at us in his cherubic way and said, "I thought you were coming alone, Mr. Richards."

"I'm representing him, Mr. Morley," I said with dignity. "I'm also representing Mrs. Richards."

Willis Morley permitted himself a cynical smile. "I'll bet. I'll wager, however, that none of your clients gets quite the personal service you give yourself."

I sighed. "A man has to eat, Mr. Morley. Is your family home?"

"I'm alone," he said impatiently. "Come in, come in."

We went through the hallway to the living room and through that to a den at the rear of the house, behind the garage. It was a warm night, and the windows were open.

The den was paneled in walnut, furnished in bright leathers and light-toned woods——real first-class California living.

As we seated ourselves, I asked, "When will Serano be here?"

"I don't know any Serano," Willis Morley said blandly.

138

He sat behind a low walnut desk.

"When I phoned you," Richards protested, "and mentioned that I'd like to see Lou Serano at the same time, you didn't say you didn't know him."

Morley smiled. "Didn't I? Is it important? I repeat, I have no idea who Lou Serano is."

I said quietly, "He's the man who sold Fidelia Richards morphine at a price about five hundred per cent above the current figure. And you're the man who gave her the money for it—at what usurious rate, Mr. Morley? Since she's been off it, she hasn't needed your money, has she?"

"My books are open to any authorized person," he said stiffly. "You can get yourself into a lot of trouble talking usury, Mr. Puma."

"Can I? When Mrs. Richards is ready to go into court and swear that when she signed a note for a thousand dollars, she only received five hundred? Each time, she only received half of the face amount of the note."

"She can swear any way she wants to," Morley said. "The papers speak for themselves, and the interest rate is plainly stated on all the notes. A discussion of discounts is far too involved for us to indulge in it tonight."

"How about a discussion of murder?" I asked him. "Are you ready for that?"

His face showed nothing. "You're not making sense," he said.

"Maybe not. You know, I got too involved in the Foy-Tampett axis to realize there was another—Serano-Morley. Serano feeding poor Fidelia the kind of stuff that only Morley would advance her money for. And then when Foy cured her, both of you suffered."

"I don't know any Serano," he said.

"Along comes Delsy," I went on, "who knows about both alliances. And so when Tampett conned Pete, here, into going after Delsy with a gun, Serano had a stake in that, too. And so did you. Serano drove Pete over and when he realized Pete was too drunk to shoot straight, he did the job. And it wasn't until this afternoon that Pete remembered that Serano had driven him to the Avalon Beach."

"I don't know what you're talking about. If this Serano

139

person is involved in murder, why aren't you looking for him?"

"We are," I said. "Call him out."

"You're being ridiculous," he said primly. "For the last time, I don't know any Lou Serano."

"Then what," I asked him quietly, "is his car doing in your garage?"

There was a long silence. Morley looked at me and I stared at him and Richards looked at the top of Morley's desk.

I said, "Serano tried to con me into believing a man named Don Ranzio was interested in Fidelia's welfare and Lou was working for him. Ranzio told me this afternoon that that was a lie. Do you want to bring him out now?"

Morley's voice was almost a whisper. "What do you want from me?"

I said, "I want you to cancel all that paper you hold on Mrs. Richards. I want you to give me Serano for the law. And what you figure my services might be worth . . ." I shrugged.

"Blackmail," he said.

"Call it an adjustment of accounts. And what's a little money to a man like you? Give us Serano and get out of town for a couple weeks. Everything will be all smoothed out by the time you get back."

His eyes left mine and flicked toward a closet door. I followed his gaze and saw that the door was partly ajar. I moved my chair around so that my back wouldn't be toward that door.

Willis Morley's blue eyes came back to examine Richards and me thoughtfully. His voice was calm. "You've put together a story, but it's all guesses, isn't it? You haven't got a thing to take into court."

"I've got Pete here to put the finger on Lou Serano. And Mrs. Richards to explain about your financial shenanigans." I paused. "And down at the Venice Station, Lieutenant Lusk has an incriminating fingerprint he hasn't matched up, one that was picked up in the place where Tampett died."

His voice was less calm. "Fingerprint?"

I nodded. "It could be Lou Serano's, though I should

140

think Lou's prints would be on file some place. Tell me, did he take a cut of your business with Mrs. Richards? And then did you take a cut of his?"

Again, he glanced toward the closet door.

"We don't do business?" I asked.

"I don't think you have anything to sell," he said.

"I've got my story, and Serano's presence here makes the story look halfway acceptable to the police. That and the stories of Mr. and Mrs. Richards are half a case." I stood up. "The fingerprint Lieutenant Lusk is holding could be the clincher." I reached for the phone on his desk. "We'll call him."

His chubby hand came over to press on the cradle switch. "Just one second."

I stood there holding a dead phone in my hand while Willis Morley bent over the desk, staring up at me.

And now the door finally opened and Lou Serano came out. He was smiling. He didn't look at all frightened.

He nodded toward Pete Richards. "Send the amateur out. Let him wait in the car."

"Just a minute—" Richards protested.

"Go ahead," I told him. "You're not going to be cheated. Wait in the car."

Richards went out, grumbling. A fine piece of acting.

Lou looked at Willis Morley like a cat looking at a goldfish. "A fingerprint, eh? Before, it was just my word against yours, but now there's a fingerprint." He smiled at me. "Joe, there'll be plenty for all, won't there? We'll all get rich off little Willis Morley. We've got an annuity, haven't we?"

I stared between them and settled on Lou. "You mean *he* killed Tampett?"

"Who else? I saw him leave there, a couple hours before I went back. When I went back, Tampett was dead. That was when you found me there."

Willis Morley said nothing, his eyes moving craftily between us.

"But of course," I explained to Lou, "Morley here probably also knows that you killed Brian Delsy."

Lou shook his head. "Nothing of the kind. We know who killed Delsy. He's sitting out in the car. You weren't conning me with his story about his memory returning.

141

That boy was so drunk he didn't know his own name."

"You ought to know," I said. "You were with him, weren't you? You drove him."

"If I did, do you think I'd admit it? Joe, I'm clean and you're clean and who's got anything on Richards? Nobody but you. So that gives us Willis to pluck, and when Richards gets back into the big time, we've got him." He paused, studying me. "And maybe Fidelia?"

"Three rich people, more or less," I said thoughtfully.

"Right," he said. "And a couple sharpies like us. Hell, in a couple years, we could retire on that kind of money."

"Sure," I said, and smiled at smiling Lou. "Sure," I repeated, *"but who needs you?"*

The smile left Lou's face. Behind his low desk, Willis stirred and looked at me hopefully. His hand moved slowly toward a desk drawer.

"Willis has got the money," I explained. "And the reputation. Who's going to believe a pusher? You haven't got a chance, Lou. Richards will nail you for the Delsy kill and Willis knows you killed Tampett."

Lou's voice was tight. "You're kidding. What kind of gag is this?"

"Face reality," I told him scornfully. "Am I going to buck the money? Don't I always ride with the money?"

He nodded, his face vacant and slack, looking between us, studying us. And then suddenly there was a gun in his hand. He nodded toward Morley. "Get over next to him, Joe, and let's start talking sense."

I moved slowly, putting my bulk between Morley and Serano, giving Morley time to open that drawer. By the time I was standing next to him, his right hand was in his lap and the gun in it was facing Lou Serano through the wide knee-hole of the desk.

From where he stood, Lou couldn't see the gun. "And now," he said, "who needs Puma?"

"Morley needs me," I said. "He can't trust you. Nobody can trust you, Lou. You won't stay bought. Who can trust a pusher?"

"That's right," Morley said. "A pusher and a killer. A man would be a damned fool to ride with you, Lou Serano."

The gun in Lou's hand swung from a point between

142

us to center on Willis Morley. He wasn't going to shoot, I felt sure; but his face was malevolent and Willis was nervous.

Willis was an amateur at this, almost, with only one killing on his record, and he had reason to thoroughly mistrust Lou Serano, a man whose loyalty remained constant only to himself.

The little .32 in Willis Morley's hand went *splat, splat, splat* and Lou went stumbling backwards, blood seeping out from his stomach. I ducked for the shelter of the desk.

From the open window behind Willis, Mel Braun shouted sharply, "Drop the gun, Morley. You're covered all around."

Loepke sat behind the battered desk, wearily getting the reports from Braun and from the hospital, where Locker was with Serano.

The room was small and full of cigarette smoke. The light over Sergeant Loepke had a green shade and it gave his taut face a green pallor.

"The print matches," he told me. "Morley was there, all right, and he admits it. But now he's talking self-defense. He says Tampett tried to blackmail him because of his tie-up with Serano. He laughed at him, started to leave, and Tampett pulled a gun. They struggled, and the gun went off. Self-defense."

I smiled. "He probably watches those old movies on TV. But what have you got? Two witnesses and one of them dead. And Morley has the money to hire the best attorneys."

"I've got Serano," he said. "Dying at the hospital. I guess he must have been religious, once. He's making a full confession."

"Is he really dying, Sergeant," I asked, "or is he just being led to believe he's dying?"

He glared at me and said nothing.

"And Richards?" I asked.

"We're holding him for a while." He stood up and stretched, rubbing the back of his neck. "Well, Joe, I didn't want to go along with it, did I? I apologize—and *thanks*."

"You're an honest man, Sergeant," I said. "You don't owe anybody in the world an apology for that. Good night and good luck."

Fid lin was standing in the corridor near the front door and I said, "I could use a drink or two. How about you?"

She shook her head, her eyes distant. "I'm waiting for Pete. He'll need me tonight."

I went down to my dusty car. The night was clear and the stars bright. I didn't want to go home. I started the engine and pointed my weary steed toward the flavorful coffee and lower middle-class home of Mrs. Arnold Foy. We would be lonely together.

Printed in the United States
By Bookmasters